M000206302

WARRIOR PRINCE

MLR Press Authors

Featuring a roll call of some of the best writers of gay erotica and mysteries today!

Maura Anderson	LB Gregg
Victor J. Banis	Drewey Wayne Gunn
Jeanne Barrack	Samantha Kane
Laura Baumbach	Kiernan Kelly
Alex Beecroft	JL Langley
Sarah Black	Josh Lanyon
Ally Blue	Clare London
J.P. Bowie	William Maltese
P.A. Brown	Gary Martine
James Buchanan	ZA Maxfield
Jordan Castillo Price	Jet Mykles
Kit Cheng	L. Picaro
Kirby Crow	Neil Plakcy
Dick D.	Luisa Prieto
Jason Edding	AM Riley
Angela Fiddler	George Seaton
Dakota Flint	Jardonn Smith
Kimberly Gardner	Caro Soles
Storm Grant	Richard Stevenson
Amber Green	Claire Thompson

Check out titles, both available and forthcoming, at
www.mlrpress.com

WARRIOR PRINCE

J.P. BOWIE

mlrpress

This book is a work of fiction. Names, characters, places, and incidents either are products of the author's imagination or are used fictitiously. Any resemblance to actual events or locales or persons, living or dead, is entirely coincidental.

Copyright 2009 by J.P. Bowie

All rights reserved, including the right of reproduction in whole or in part in any form.

Published by
MLR Press, LLC
3052 Gaines Waterport Rd.
Albion, NY 14411

Visit ManLoveRomance Press, LLC on the Internet:
www.mlrpress.com

Cover Art by Deana C. Jamroz
Editing by Kris Jacen
Printed in the United States of America.

ISBN# 978-1-934531-88-4

First Edition
2009

PROLOGUE

Three years before this story begins, two lovers were torn apart by circumstances too great for them to overcome. A young Capuan tutor, in love with a rebel slave, a fugitive from the rebellion led by the legendary Spartacus, was forced to acknowledge that their future together was an impossible one. Sadly, he moved through the days, months and years, spending time with his friends, caring for his mother and sisters, tutoring his students—all the while hiding from everyone his broken heart.

From the moment he first set eyes on Callistus, the Gaul, young Lucius Tullius was in love. Though fate had set them at opposite ends of society's spectrum, their paths crossed more than once, and their attraction for one another could not be denied. Throwing aside all caution, Lucius risked scandal and deprivation in order to reach Callistus in the camp where the soldiers of Spartacus were entrenched. There, among the rebel forces, the love Callistus and Lucius felt for one another was consummated. However short lived their time of passion was, neither man could ever forget the sensuous delight it had brought them.

When the Army led by Spartacus was finally crushed by the legions of Rome, Callistus, one of the few survivors and on the run from those who would destroy him, could not leave without holding Lucius in his arms one last time. Though the threat of capture was real, he found his way to Lucius, who, believing him killed in a prior battle, was overjoyed to find his lover alive. Their night of love was made bittersweet by the knowledge that in the morning Callistus would have to depart, forever.

And so, for three long years, Lucius has mourned the loss of his lover, hoping that somehow, somewhere, they might be reunited. A hope that, with each passing year, seems to grow more and more unattainable, until...

CHAPTER I

LUCIUS

I stood to one side of my mother, watching the wedding ceremony with a satisfied smile. This was the third wedding I had attended in the past four months, but it was the one that I had looked forward to with the most anticipation.

My long time friend and confidant, Turio, who now stood somewhere behind me among the crowd of well wishers, had been the first to tie the knot earlier in the year. His betrothed, Dido, had finally persuaded him that he should make an honest woman of her. Shortly thereafter, my sister Lucia had married Cassius, a wealthy merchant's son. And now today, my darling widowed mother was marrying Gaius Venicius, an older, but still spry member of the Senate.

Apart from the fact that I was happy to see my mother remarried after close to six years of widowhood, I also felt as though a huge burden had been lifted from my shoulders. Ever since my father died, leaving virtually no money for his family's welfare, I had been the one they had looked to as the provider of food and clothing, and a roof over their heads... a task I had never considered myself capable of. Yet somehow I had managed, and even though clearing my father's debts had meant giving my body for the pleasure of a corpulent Etruscan merchant, I now deemed it all worthwhile.

Pushing those thoughts to the back of my mind, I concentrated on the marriage ceremony now taking place. The traditional words of commitment were ready to be said. I smiled as my mother, looking lovely in her white dress and veil, chanted the words, "Where and when you are Gaius, then there am I, Gaia." How lucky an omen that the names recited at every wedding, regardless of the real names of the bride and groom, were actually the names of my mother and stepfather. Surely, the gods were smiling on them this day.

As the offering was made for their happiness, I caught the eye of my other friend, Petronius, who stood a little ways off with his wife, Aurelia, and their tiny daughter. Petronius, I thought with a sigh, so unhappy with his life of domesticity. How often I had listened to him bemoaning the decision he had made to marry Aurelia some years before. How much happier might he have been if he had only let his "natural" tendencies lead him to a more fulfilling life?

Ah well… sacrifices must be made by all, it seemed.

The gods knew just what my own sacrifices had cost me. The love of a man for whom I would never find an equal, no matter how long I searched and waited. Even now, standing among my friends and family on this joyous occasion, I felt the aching void that the loss of Callistus, my Gallic warrior, had brought me every day for the past three years. A heartache compounded by the fact that I could no longer discuss any part of it with any of my friends. They had thought me mad at the beginning of my infatuation with the captive Gaul—and now, after all this time, would show no patience or understanding for my continued devotion to a man long gone, and of whom I had heard not one word in all that time.

I was abruptly shaken from my melancholy thoughts at the sound of my mother's voice as she cried out for her only son to embrace her and his new father. Happily I complied, then led them to the table where a lavish dinner was to be served, before the other guests and I accompanied them to my mother's new home—a splendid villa on the outskirts of Rome that Gaius had especially built for his new bride.

If I were the jealous sort, I would almost envy my mother her happiness. Even if she would never admit it, I knew her previous marriage to my father had been a cold and lonely existence. My sisters had been too young to understand their mother's pain, but I had seen it time and time again reflected in her eyes, and my heart had gone out to her, even if she would not acknowledge my understanding of her unhappiness. Gaia, my mother, was a true Roman matron, dedicated to her husband and her family. But now, it was as if she had been liberated, and I could not but feel a deep affection and admiration for the man who had brought her this happiness.

The procession to the newlyweds' new home gave Petronius the opportunity to ride close to me. His wife and daughter were seated together in a carriage with Turio and Dido, but Petronius had made the excuse his horse needed the exercise, and now cantered alongside me, eager to talk—and make known his wishes for time alone with me later that night.

"It will be perfect," he enthused. "You will have the house all to yourself... please let me come see you later."

I sighed inwardly. As much as I loved Petronius, and had all my life, my friend's demands were not always welcome. There had been a time when I had longed for more from Petronius. A time when I had wondered if it were at all possible for the two of us to have a life together. Something that Petronius himself had negated when he had married Aurelia, telling me that to marry and raise a family was expected of every man, regardless of his feelings or longings for another life.

And now, it was to me that Petronius turned when his heart was heavy, and his need for sexual relief was too much to bear—and I found I could not turn my lifelong friend away, even though my very soul cried out for the one who had stolen my heart all those years ago.

"Won't Aurelia be looking for you after the ceremony?" I asked, glancing at my friend, who looked at me with an eagerness that I found faintly sad.

Petronius snorted. "No... she'll be abed and asleep before I can even get a foot in the door. I've told you, that's how it is every night since Portia was born. She has no wish for me, or any man, to fuck her."

"I'm sorry..." I looked ahead at my mother's new home, now illuminated with a myriad of torches lining the outside walls. "Then of course you may come to the house after..."

"Thank you, Lucius." He reached out and grasped my arm. "You, as always, have given me something to look forward to."

Our conversation was halted as the house servants ran toward us, carrying torches to light our way under the villa's impressive arched entry way and into the courtyard, where we were helped to dismount and the horses led away. Gaius, his chubby face beaming with anticipation of what the night ahead might hold, waved us forward.

"Lucius," he cried. "You must witness my carrying your dear mother over the threshold."

We walked into the midst of the invited guests and joined in the shouts of encouragement as Gaius, his face red with exertion, lifted his new bride into his arms, and wobbling slightly, passed through the portals of the villa. Inside, servants plied the guests with wine and desserts while a small group of musicians struck up a lively tune of celebration. As I looked around, I felt a degree of satisfaction that this fine house would be my mother's and my little sister's home. Little Julia was to be formally adopted by Gaius, who had wanted to include me, but I had politely declined the offer. At the age of twenty-six, I felt it better if I remained unfettered by legal adoption. That way I was free to choose the path in life I wished to pursue. Never mind that I did not know just what that should be as yet...

Turio and his wife, Dido, appeared at my side, smiles at the ready, and I knew what they were about to say before they even opened their mouths to speak. I sighed as I listened to the familiar words.

"Now then Lucius..." This from Turio, whom I felt should know better. "Isn't it about time you thought of tying the knot? Look at all your friends, and now your mother, happily married."

"Well, married anyway," I remarked, dryly.

"Turio and I are *very* happy, thank you Lucius," Dido said, with a haughty expression. "And I'm sure your mother and sister are too."

"I was thinking more of Petronius, actually." I glanced across the room to where Petronius was chatting amiably enough to some of the guests.

Dido snorted in a rather unladylike way. "Petronius makes his own trouble," she muttered. "He complains to you and Turio that Aurelia has no time for him, but she tells *me* that when she does let him into her bed, he shows very little interest."

I threw Turio an annoyed look. "You talk of this—about Petronius? The gods only know what you must say about me behind my back!"

"Now don't go getting in a twist, Lucius," Turio said, rolling his eyes. "You know we are only concerned with your welfare, and it's only right that Aurelia has someone she can confide in. Petronius never hesitates to let us know exactly what *he's* thinking."

"And here all this time, I thought he was telling us these things in confidence," I interrupted. "As, I'm sure, does he." I felt a degree of satisfaction as Turio's face reddened with discomfort.

"I'll just go and get us some more wine," he muttered, grabbing Dido's cup and practically running to the other side of the room.

"You were harsh with him," she said with a reproving look in her eyes. "He thinks the world of you, you know."

"I doubt if our friendship will suffer from my words."

"And if you want to know what we say about you," Dido continued in her haughty fashion, "we merely feel that you are wasting your life by not finding a suitable girl to marry. Isn't it time you put aside those *other* feelings you have, and settle down with a wife and family?"

The retort I had on the tip of my tongue was stayed as an arm was thrown round my shoulders and Petronius said loudly,

"Lucius, settle down with a wife and children. Surely you jest, Dido. Don't you know him at all?"

Dido looked at him through narrowed eyes. "Obviously not as well as you know him, dear Petronius."

"Nor shall you!" Petronius laughed and hugged me to him. It was apparent that he'd had a little too much wine. "Anyway, why this boring talk of settling down? We're at a wedding!"

I chuckled. "And, of course, a wedding is completely the wrong place for such conversation."

Dido smiled wanly. "I'll leave you two men to your little jokes." She accepted the cup of wine Turio had arrived with, then taking his arm, steered him toward where the bride and groom were holding court.

"Good riddance," Petronius muttered. "She's becoming old before her time, that one. She acts like she's Turio's mother instead of his wife."

"Are they happy, d'you think?" I asked, taking a cup of wine from a passing servant's tray.

"Happy enough, I dare say. Well…" He raised his own cup of wine and saluted me. "Here's to your new life as one who now has no restraints. Who is now as free as a bird, able to carouse each and every night if he so wishes, without fear of a mother's reprimand."

"My mother never reprimanded me, as well you know. It will be strange for a while I think, being alone in the house. Part of me has yearned for it, but I think I will miss my mother's fussing, and little Julia's laughter…"

"I won't let you be lonely, Lucius." Petronius' eyes were filled with longing as he gazed at me. "I will always be there when you need me."

"I know, and I thank you for that."

And it was true. In the long lonely years since Callistus and I had last been together, I had treasured Petronius' company and compassion. Occasionally, we would express our love for one another in more than just words. I knew Petronius was sex-starved at home. Aurelia, his wife, was not a sensual being, regarding sex as a necessary act in order to produce children. Petronius had told me that as often as he had tried to bring her delight in their coupling, he had at best left her unmoved, and at worst induced a bitter tirade from her about the perversity of men's needs.

I had at one time been enamored of Petronius, and would have welcomed him into my bed without exception, but now… The memory of the ecstasy Callistus had brought me made my union with Petronius feel almost a betrayal of the man I loved. Still, I could not find it in my heart to deny Petronius the occasional comfort he craved, and when I was honest with myself, I would admit that his affectionate kisses and caresses were of a great solace to me also.

Seeing the need in Petronius now, I squeezed his arm, then raising my voice to be heard over the clamor of the wedding guests' chatter, I exclaimed, "Friends, as the proud son of my mother, Gaia, now the beautiful bride of Gaius Venicius, I ask you to join with me in wishing them both long life, and happiness, always."

I paused as everyone yelled their approval.

"To Gaius, my congratulations on winning such a wonderful woman as my mother. To my little sister, Julia, I wish you much happiness, my dear, in your new home. And to all of you, thank you for attending and joining us in this happy celebration. Now, perhaps it is time to leave the newlyweds alone. May the gods bless this union, and grant them love and happiness for the rest of their lives together."

A round of applause rang out, then the guests gathered round to wish my mother and her new husband good fortune, and a goodnight. I sought out my little sister, who was going to spend the first night of her life not in her own bed. As I expected, Julia was not at all nervous or put out by these changes in her life.

"You must come and see my room, Lucius," she said, gripping my hand and pulling me away from the throng. We laughed together as we ran down the marbled hall where she proudly displayed her very own special domain. "Is it not beautiful, Lucius?"

And indeed it is, I thought, gazing at the fine furnishings and delicately painted pink walls. Much grander than her little room at home. I felt a momentary twinge of sadness that my little sister might not look forward to spending too many nights with me, once she was used to this luxury.

"It's beautiful," I said, putting my hand on her head and stroking her hair gently. "A room fit for a young lady such as yourself."

"Are you sad?" Julia asked, looking up at me with big eyes.

"A little... and happy too, for you and for Mother."

"You'll visit often, won't you?"

"Yes, and you will come and see me in our old home."

"Why won't you come and live here, Lucius? Gaius is nice and..."

"Yes," I interrupted. "He is nice, but I must find my own way in life now. I cannot rely on another man's wealth to support me."

"Why not?" Julia's face crinkled with bewilderment at my words.

I sighed. It was obvious my little sister was already becoming used to her stepfather's wealth and generosity.

"Because that is not my way. I am a man, and must make my own way."

"If you say so... Look at the new dress Gaius gave me yesterday..."

✳ ✳ ✳ ✳ ✳

I strolled slowly through the courtyard outside my home, glad that Rufus, my manservant, had already lit the outside lamps. The warmth that the flickering flames spread across the neatly tended garden helped a little to dispel the gloom that had fallen upon me since taking leave of my mother and Julia. For a few minutes I was content to stay outside, filling my nostrils with the scents from the jasmine and gardenia bushes that grew in abundance everywhere. I sat on a bench near the entrance to the house and let my mind be flooded with the bittersweet memories that thoughts of Callistus always brought me.

This evening, perhaps because of the happiness I'd been witness to earlier, these memories seemed even more sharply painful than usual. For the hundredth time, I wondered why I went on hoping that one day Callistus would appear before me, just as he had done on that night almost three years ago. The night when, on the run from Roman legions after the defeat of the servile army commanded by Spartacus, he had come to say farewell to me, to tell me he loved me, and to spend one last night holding me in his arms.

My mind flew back to that moment when thoughts of Callistus had proven too much. I had risen from my bath, and after hastily drying myself, flung on a robe and walked outside into the warm night air. I stood in the garden trying to calm my mind that seethed with unsettling emotions.

Perhaps a cup of wine…

From the stables came the sound of a soft whinny. Belenus… Frowning, I made my way across the yard to the darkened stables. Pushing open the door, I walked toward his stall. My heart froze in my chest as in the moonlit shadows I made out the shape of a tall figure standing by the horse's side.

"Step away, thief!" I yelled, my hand going instinctively to my belt for my knife, which of course I was not carrying.

"Lucius…" The voice was hoarse and weary, yet unmistakable.

"Callistus!" Delirious joy made me clumsy as I stumbled forward into his arms. "The gods be praised. I thought you dead. In the forum, they said you had died at Mutina. I knew you could not be dead. I willed it so…"

His mouth on mine stilled my babbling. His arms crushed me to him in an embrace that threatened to break every rib in my body. I clung to him, my heart pounding as I reveled in the feel of his strong, hard body pressed against mine. The roughness of his beard, the stale smell of his clothes told me he had been on the road for many days. Despite my exhilaration, I knew he needed caring for.

"Come," I whispered. "Let me take you inside. You need to rest, I think."

Gratefully, he nodded, letting me lead him from the stable back to the house, and my room, where I quietly closed the door, in case my mother or one of the servants overheard us. In the light cast by the lamp near my bed, he looked gaunt and exhausted. His clothes hung about him in tatters, his hair was dull and matted, and his eyes held a melancholy I could not bear to see.

"Oh, Callistus…" I laid my head on his chest and held him close. His hands stroked my hair, and then he raised my face to his and kissed me again, and again. "How I have longed for this moment," I whispered against his lips. "I have prayed every day for the chance to see you again."

His smile was grim. "And I come to you like this," he said, his voice still hoarse. "Hardly the fearless gladiator you once admired."

"Hush," I murmured, pulling at his ragged tunic. "You must bathe, and I will fetch you food and wine." He stood still as I undressed him, my hands straying over his naked chest and muscular back. There were scars on his body I had not seen before, a bad one across his lower back. "You are injured…"

He shrugged. "It is healing, but the coward who dealt the blow was not so lucky."

"I will put some salve on it once you have bathed," I said, leading him to the bath. He let out a long sigh as he settled into the warm water. He closed his eyes for a moment, an expression of bliss flickering on his face. I turned to go, but his hand on mine stayed me.

"You must tell me if this is not convenient for you," he said, softly.

"Not convenient?" I sat on the edge of the bath and kissed his lips. "It is everything I have longed for, my love."

I crept into the kitchen, silently piling some bread, cheese and olives onto a plate, then filled a jug with wine. I rummaged through the small chest of "useful things" my mother kept and found a small jar of salve. When I returned he was washing his hair. He leaned back in the bath and studied me, a half smile on his noble face.

"You look well," he said, "and as handsome as ever."

"*Thank you.*" *I poured him a cup of wine, which he drank down in one long swallow, and then he stood, the water coursing from his magnificent body in streaming rivulets. I could not take my eyes from him. The very sight of him, so close to me again, fired my blood with desire. I gave him a towel and watched as he carefully dried himself.*

"*Do you have something I can wear?*" *he asked, wrapping the towel about his hips.*

"*It will be a tight fit,*" *I said, fetching a tunic from my bed chest. "Before you dress, I have brought some salve for your wound." He stood quietly while I applied it to the cut on his lower back. As I finished, I could not resist letting my hands stray over the curve of his muscular buttocks.*

He chuckled from the depths of his chest. "Is that part of the treatment, Doctor Lucius?" he asked, turning to me, an expression of mock reproof on his handsome face. He already looked ten times better than when I had first seen him in the stable.

"*It could be,*" *I replied cheekily, letting myself be pulled into his arms. I opened my robe to feel his nakedness against my own bare skin, and the sensation was almost overpowering in its intensity. I clung to him, then remembered my well-intentioned resolution to care for him first, before inflicting my carnal desire upon him.*

"*You must be starving,*" *I whispered, half hoping he would deny it.*

"*It has been some time since last I ate,*" *he admitted, so I took his hand and led him to where I had left the tray of food.*

"*Come now, eat and have some more wine.*"

Smiling, he sat by me and pulled a hunk of bread from the loaf I had brought. This he devoured quickly, along with the cheese and olives. I poured some wine for him and myself and was happy to watch him eat, letting him enjoy what must have been his first meal in several days.

"*How did you know where to find me?*" *I asked him finally.*

"*Your slave, Rollus, gave me the directions.*"

"*Rollus...*" *He had left our household to join with Spartacus. "Is he well? Where is he?*"

"He is well. He was with me at the end, one of the few not captured by the Romans. He went back to his family. I hope you don't mind that I did not bring him back to you."

"No, no of course not. I'm just happy he survived." I bit my lip as his eyes clouded. *"How terrible was it?"*

"It was a terrible mistake, Lucius," he replied, his face pained at the memory of it. *"Spartacus seemed to have lost direction in the last few months of his life. We should have crossed into Gaul after we defeated Cassius Longinus at Mutina, but so many of the men wanted more plunder, more spoils—and there was so much to take from the rich estates. I tried to reason with some of them, but they would not listen, and Spartacus bowed to the majority.*

"I was so tempted to leave, as others had done, but he had lost his closest friend, and I felt it would have been a betrayal to leave him at that moment. I know he was grateful for my decision, and I suppose all would have been well if the men who had offered him passage to Sicily had not reneged on their promise. Instead of ships to save us, the gods sent legions to destroy us. I think we had run out of their favor. I also think that Spartacus had given up the fight. His leadership at that point was uninspired, his battle decisions faulty. I tried to steer him on the right course, but he would not listen. We fought well, Lucius, but this time we were simply overwhelmed."

"I am just grateful that the gods spared your life," I said, taking his hand.

"The gods have the power to pick and choose, I suppose," he said, with some bitterness. *"But there are times when I question their unfairness in matters of life and death. It seems as if they smiled on us for a while, and then when they grew bored, decided to end the game, taking away all that we had fought so hard for."*

"The gods can be cruel," I agreed. *"All this time I thought you were dead. For months now, I have mourned you, but I am ready to exalt them once more, now that they have brought you back to me."*

"Lucius…" He raised my hand to his lips, and kissed it gently. *"You know I must leave. It would only be a matter of time before word spreads that you are harboring a runaway slave—and more than that, a fugitive from the servile army. You know the punishment for that is death. I cannot endanger you and your family."*

In the flickering light of my bedside lamp, his skin and hair had taken on a golden glow, and my heart ached at the sight of his beauty. Of course, I knew that what he said was correct, and in truth I would not willfully endanger my family either. My dilemma was that I could not bear to lose him again.

"Then I must go with you," I said.

"No!" His reply was curt. "There is too much danger involved, Lucius. We would be hunted across all Italia."

"I cannot let you go, Callistus," I cried, throwing myself into his arms. "Don't you know how much I love you? I cannot live without you now, not after finding that you are still alive. Please take me with you!"

He held me pressed tightly against his hard chest. "Lucius," he murmured into my hair. "You must understand…"

"Then why," I sobbed, "why did you come here? To torment me by showing me that you still live, only to leave me again? Why did you do this? Why did you not just keep going, until you reached where you really want to be?"

"Because I love you, Lucius." He held my face between his hands, and gazed into my eyes as he spoke the words I had wanted to hear since the first day we met. "I love you," he said again. "And I could not go without seeing you once more. Without telling you what has been in my heart for so long."

I fell into his arms, holding him until I thought my heart would burst. My mind exulted to the echo of his words—I love you, Lucius. Never had words more beautiful been spoken to me. I kissed his chest, then lifted my head and looked at him with what I prayed was sincerity.

"I know you are right," I said, hoping the gods would forgive my lie. "But know this, Callistus, the one man who has stirred my selfish heart to encompass something that is real and meaningful, I will never forget you, nor stop loving you. Wherever our lives take us, you will remain in my heart, forever."

His lips captured mine in a kiss that made my senses reel. He stood, lifting me into his arms, and I clung to him, encircling his hips with my legs, his neck with my arms. I rejoiced in the feel of his hard, throbbing manhood that wedged itself between my buttocks. Our eyes locked upon one another; he shifted so that the head of his cock pushed past my unresisting sphincter, and I bore down on him, driving that hard living flesh inside me, gasping at the pain, but enraptured by the thrill and ecstasy of our mutual passion. He held me like this, his hands supporting me as I moved to an erotic rhythm, up and down on his pulsing shaft. I covered his face with my kisses, saying his name over and over, telling him how much I loved him, and how the memory of this moment would live with me forever.

Still deep within me, he lowered me onto my bed, his lips searing the flesh on my chest with his kisses, his arms enfolding me, crushing me to his body as if he would never let me go. And oh, how I prayed that he would not. Through my ecstasy at being in his arms once more, I sensed that this would be but a swift and bittersweet reconciliation. Those thoughts were momentarily eradicated as he buried his face in my chest, his lips and tongue worrying at my nipples, causing me to moan aloud at the sensations he aroused in me. Grasping his hair in my hands I forced his face to mine. Our kiss was long and deep. Locked within the strength of his arms, I inhaled his smell, and his taste.

"Lucius, my sweet Lucius," he murmured, his lips never leaving mine.

My hands stroked and caressed the smooth skin that covered his muscular back, then reached to cup his buttocks and pull him ever deeper inside me. I heard him growl with pleasure. His thrusts became longer and faster. He grasped my erection in his hand, propelling me toward my orgasm. My breath quickened as I felt liquid fire spread through my loins. I clung to him, gasping his name as I lost control. His mouth closed over mine as every muscle in his body stiffened with the onslaught of his own orgasm. I could feel his hot seed erupt inside me, filling me with his love. Never had I been more complete.

We lay still and quiet afterward, his lips on my brow, his fingertips gently caressing my chest. I knew that in my lifetime I would never feel as happy, nor as sad, again.

I felt my breath catch in my throat as those memories flooded my mind and conjured up a vision of the handsome Gaul who had captivated me from the very first time I saw him. A slave, caged in the marketplace, but with the noble bearing of a prince. I remembered, too, how Turio had derided my all-too-apparent attraction for the captive Gaul, and how my friends had tried to dissuade me from my obsession with him. They had thought me mad, and even I had begun to think that perhaps I was, until the day when he and I had come face to face, and he had held me in his arms and won my love forever.

Never would I forget that first moment when his lips met mine in a kiss that had set my senses reeling, and my body on fire with a passion that had never abated. The memory of the time we had spent together making love would live with me for all time, and diminish any other moment spent in another's arms. Sometimes I would curse him for having given me a taste of a rapture I could never again experience. But then I would immerse myself in the memories of his smile, of his strength and of his sweetness of nature that had brought me from mere infatuation to a deep, abiding love of the man he truly was. During the two years that passed from the day of our first meeting in the market place until the army he served in under Spartacus was defeated, we were alone together a matter of only three times. And yet those times have lived on in my mind and in my heart as memories of the sweetest moments of my life.

"Can I get you some refreshment, Master Lucius?" Rufus' soft voice at my shoulder brought me back from my reverie.

"Some wine, Rufus, thank you," I said, giving myself a good shake. "Master Petronius will be here shortly."

"At once, Master."

I followed him indoors, allowing him to free me of the heavy ceremonial toga I had worn to the wedding. The light tunic I wore underneath felt like freedom after the weight of the thick and cumbersome material. I stretched, then rubbed my arms where the toga had irritated my skin.

"Lucius?"

I turned at the sound of my friend's voice. "Come on in, Petronius. Rufus is bringing us some wine." Petronius had shed his toga also, and his smooth, olive hued skin shone in the lamplight. He is so handsome, I thought. Even now, after all these years, he still has the look of the boy about him. Petronius, for his part, was staring at me with a gleam in his eye.

He was about to grab me when Rufus entered, carrying our wine.

"Good evening, Master Petronius."

"Ah, Rufus. Efficient as always," Petronius said, winking at me. "I wish my household slaves were half as good as you."

I frowned and gave Rufus a look of apology. I disliked having him referred to as a slave. Ever since my conversations with Callistus, I had begun to respect a man's right to freedom. Even though Rufus was in my service, I considered him more a companion than a servant. My previous manservant, Rollus, had left me to join with the servile army led by Spartacus. He had gone with my blessing, and the wish I could have joined him. Callistus had seen him safely home after the slave armies were defeated, and Spartacus slain in the final battle.

Rufus had come to us after his mistress, a friend of my mother's, had died. He was an older man, and had known no other life than service. We had taken him in, but from the start I wanted him to feel a part of the household, not just a servant. Foolish though it may seem, I felt that Callistus would have been proud of me for that.

As we sat on my bed together, Petronius took my hand and kissed it gently. "I do so love you for this, Lucius. You are the only friend who truly understands me."

I gazed into his light hazel-colored eyes and smiled at the sincerity I saw there. Even if this was not what I really wanted from our friendship, even if my heart and mind belonged to another, what harm was there in giving him some comfort, and the warmth of my arms on occasion?

With one hand, he massaged the nape of my neck while the other stroked my thigh. I could see from the tenting in front of his tunic that he was in great need of my ministrations. I slipped off the bed and knelt in front of him, burrowing my head between his thighs and taking the head of his cock into my mouth. He fell back with a groan of relief, stroking the sides of my face as I sucked on him, pulling his hot flesh into the depths of my throat.

"Lucius," he moaned. I paused for a moment to strip him of his tunic and shuck mine off at the same time. Impatiently he grabbed me, threw me on my back and went down on me like a hungry animal. His feverish need was infectious, and soon we were rolling about on the bed, our mouths on each other's cocks, bringing each other to a noisy climax that left us spent, sweaty and, for myself, faintly exhilarated.

"Oh, Lucius," he said finally.

"Oh, Petronius," I replied. We chuckled together, then I rose to get our cups of wine. He took his with a kiss of thanks, and we lay together quietly for a time, each lost in our separate thoughts.

"Aurelia is with child again," he said after a time.

I raised my head to look at him with surprise. "But you said..."

"She said she wanted another child, so I was allowed in until she was sure."

"How can you stand it?" I asked.

"How can *you* stand it?" he countered.

"What d'you mean?"

"You know, this pining for the man you know will never return to you."

I felt my face grow hot. "I hope you do not share these thoughts with Turio and Dido. Those two are inveterate gossips."

"Oh, I know what they say about my marriage to Aurelia. Dido and my wife are often in each other's company. Women talk of things we men show more restraint over."

I fixed him with narrowed eyes. "I hope that means you have not discussed my 'pining,' as you put it, with them."

"Turio said something..."

"Oh, for Juno's sake, Petronius. I will not be the object of pity in the eyes of my friends!"

"Who said we pity you?"

"Right, more than like you're all laughing about it. By the gods, and you're supposed to be my friend!"

"I am your friend, and I love you, Lucius. Unlike Dido and Turio, I don't think you should be looking for a wife."

"Well, that's something, I suppose."

"It would mean you would have less time for me," he said, grinning over his wine cup at me.

I resisted the inclination to slap him, but let him see I was not happy with him. Of course, then he sidled over to me and started kissing my neck.

"Forgive my selfishness, Lucius," he mumbled between kisses.

I swatted at him, but laughed at the same time. "I suppose I am being ridiculous," I said, sitting up. "Look at me. Almost in my twenty-seventh year, and still languishing over the love of a man I can never have. What an idiot you must all think I am."

"But a handsome idiot," Petronius murmured, his lips still on my neck. I looked down at his crotch. He was hard again. I suppose I should have been flattered that, after all these years of friendship, I could still keep him horny.

CHAPTER II

Life without my family close by proceeded surprisingly as usual. Of course, I had my teaching to keep me occupied in the day time, my preparation for classes to attend to at night, and so my time for socializing was limited to the weekends and the occasional night when Turio or Petronius would visit— sometimes together, sometimes alone.

The invitation to dinner at the home of Venel Papni took me by surprise. Papni was an Etruscan shipping merchant of enormous wealth—and even more enormous girth. Some years before, when I was in dire straits financially and feared for my family's welfare, I sold myself—there is no other word for it, really—to Papni to clear the debts my father had left us. The memory of it still fills me with shame. Although Papni himself was easy enough to please, my company being more what he craved in the end, the idea of prostituting myself was not something I lived with easily. However, the merchant and I had remained friends since then, and on occasion would dine together.

I had not heard from him in some considerable time, and had thought him finally bored with my company, so his invitation, as I said, came as a surprise. I sent Rufus with a reply saying I would be delighted to see him at his home on the night indicated on the invitation, and thought no more of it until the morning of the day I was expected.

Then I panicked. I had nothing to wear! Papni's guests were all sure to be immensely wealthy, therefore wearing the finest of togas and robes. I surveyed my poor collection of mostly threadbare togas; the only one being in presentable condition the one I wore to my mother's wedding. I was going to look like the poor relation—which of course, I was. Ah well, Papni knew my circumstances better than most, yet he still invited me. Perhaps my best tunic and a light cloak would suffice; it was a lovely warm day, and the night promised to be balmy. Better without the heavy weight of a toga.

I took some extra time readying myself for the inspection I was sure would follow my arrival. If that sounds just a trifle arrogant, it just so happened that I knew very well the kind of guests Papni entertained—mostly old lechers who, despite the fact I am no longer a boy, would still find the occasion to rub against me, or stroke my arm as they engaged me in conversation. The only reason I went to these gatherings was because I felt grateful to Papni. He had helped me out of a nasty situation, and even though I had fulfilled my part of the bargain, he had not been as obnoxious as he could have been, given the circumstances.

✖ ✖ ✖ ✖ ✖

I entered his sumptuous villa through the cleverly designed atrium. The first time I visited Papni for the purpose of clearing the family debt, the gentle murmur of the fountain had calmed my jumpy nerves. I stood there for a moment, once again intrigued by its musical cadences, before entering the main room crowded with Papni's many guests.

"Ah, Lucius…" He descended upon me in all his vastness, hugging me to his bountiful bosom and laying a smacking kiss on my forehead. He smelled of some exotic spice—I thought it a bit overpowering, but the night was young, and he was prone to perspiring heavily. "Come, have some wine with me. There is a young man I wish you to meet."

Papni always had a young man for me to meet on these occasions. One night when I was more in my cups than I should have been, I told him of my heartache over losing Callistus. Ever since then, he had been trying to find me the perfect partner, as he put it, and failing miserably at the task, much to his frustration. As many times as I told him I was not interested in finding a replacement for my lost love, he would not listen. With a smile of thanks, I accepted a goblet of wine from one of his winsome, almost nude, male servants.

"Over there, see?" Papni, whispering as if to a co-conspirator, indicated a young man in an officer's uniform. "His name is Flavius Sedonius, high-born of a family from Pompeii, and a *tribune* in the Imperial Army."

At the moment that I looked over to where the young officer was standing talking with a mixed group of men and women, he chose that same precise moment to glance over at Papni and myself. Our eyes met, and he smiled and nodded. Out of politeness, I nodded in acknowledgement.

Beside me, Papni squealed with delight. "By the goddess Thesan, she who bestows love on all mankind, I knew you would both make a match!"

"Make a match? I have not yet said one word to the man."

"But you showed some interest."

"I was being polite."

"He's coming over!"

"By the gods…" I bit my tongue as the tribune approached, and I had to admit, he was definitely a cut above all the others with whom Papni had tried to interest me. He was not tall, my height only, but his body showed a power and confidence few men could equal. His coal-black hair was cut close to his scalp, and his eyes were a vivid blue. It was his eyes that made my heart lurch in my chest. If I had seen nothing more but his eyes, I would have sworn I was gazing at Callistus, if only for an instant. I felt my wine goblet tremble in my hand as he smiled at me and held out his in greeting.

"Tribune Sedonius…" Papni could hardly contain his delight at introducing us. "May I present Lucius Tullius, a very dear friend of mine, and an able scholar and tutor."

"A pleasure," he said, grasping my forearm in his warm hand.

"Mine also," I murmured, returning his grip. His arm felt hard and strong in my hand, and in my mind's eye I could see him on the battlefield, proud and unafraid of the enemy before him. "You have returned recently from a campaign?" I asked, trying to ignore Papni's grinning visage.

"Yes, in Gaul," he replied. "Those devils just won't agree to the terms we set out for them."

I felt my chest tighten at his words. He'd been in Gaul, possibly facing Callistus in battle.

"Are you all right?" he asked. "You've turned quite pale."

"Oh, I'm sorry..." My mind raced for some excuse. "Ah... I'm a little tired from preparing for so many classes these last few weeks."

"You should eat something, Lucius," Papni said, steering us both to the dining table, a meaty paw on both our shoulders. "Tribune Sedonius will keep you company while I attend my other guests." With that he lumbered off, leaving me alone with Sedonius.

"Again, I'm sorry, Tribune..."

"Don't be, and it's Flavius, by the way." He took my arm and led me to a couch by the table. "Our host is right, you should eat something." He sat by me and smiled into my eyes. "The lark's tongues in aspic are quite delicious."

"Just some bread and cheese, I think." I helped myself from the food massed on the table.

"A soldier's rations," he said, reaching for an apple. His hand brushed mine and lingered for a moment, his fingertips caressing the back of my hand. I felt a prickle of desire in my loins, and hastily pulled back from his touch.

His smile did not falter, but he shifted away from me just slightly. I felt the need to apologize... again. "I'm sorry, Flavius. I'm a little on edge tonight. You talked of Gaul, how terrible is it there?"

"Terrible enough. The Gauls are a hard enemy to beat."

"They are fighting for their homeland, of course," I said quietly.

"Yes, they are, and bravely too. Their one major weakness, though, is that they cannot combine their tribes. There's a lot of infighting among the tribal chiefs. They are called kings. If they ever joined forces and made one big army, they would be almost invincible. Fortunately for us, they have not accomplished that. It will be their undoing, in the end."

As I listened to him, I thought of Callistus and his possible standing among the tribes. I would have thought he would see the sense of a union among the various tribes. He had told me that once back home he could raise an army that would halt the Roman legions in their tracks.

"Have there been setbacks?"

"Oh, indeed. As I told you, they are a hard enemy to beat—and well led at times. Only recently, we were forced to give up what we had taken from them. Their determination to win back their land, and the bravery of their leader, won the day for them."

"Their leader?"

"Yes, a big handsome fellow with hair like wind-blown wheat. When all seemed lost, he plunged in among my soldiers, urging his men to follow. My men fell before him, and were scattered before we could regroup."

I stared at him in silence for a long moment, my mind trying to deal with what he had just told me. He could only be talking about Callistus. In my eagerness to hear more, I grabbed his arm.

"What became of their leader? Did you see him again?"

Flavius' eyes widened with surprise, no doubt taken aback at my sudden interest in the Gallic leader.

"Why no," he replied. "As I said we were forced to retreat, and the rest of my day was spent explaining our defeat to my superior officers."

"Oh, of course," I mumbled, releasing his arm. "Please excuse my lack of concern for you and your men. It was just that there used to be a gladiator here in Capua, a Gaul like the one you just described. He was a part of the rebellion led by Spartacus. I thought perhaps it was he... He was quite the favorite here in Capua for a time," I added lamely.

Flavius continued to gaze at me, his expression still slightly puzzled by my reaction. "Well," he said finally. "He certainly showed great courage. Perhaps his days in the arena helped to hone his fighting skills."

"Oh, he was a great warrior before then," I blurted. "It took ten men to hold him before he was taken into captivity!"

"Indeed." Flavius regarded me coolly. "Your admiration for an enemy warrior is a trifle misplaced, don't you think? He was responsible for the deaths of many of our fine soldiers."

"Again, I must apologize. I must sound unpatriotic, which, of course, I am not. I expect I'm getting my memory of the gladiator confused with the reality of what he really is—our enemy." I hated myself for what I had just said. It seemed to me a betrayal of the man I loved, but I didn't want to alienate Flavius. The kernel of an idea was beginning to form in my mind, and he might just be very useful to me, if I decided to go through with it.

Flavius upended his wine cup and gave me rueful smile. "Empty..." He summoned one of the wine servants over who refilled his goblet, and mine. "Well, Lucius..." Flavius took a long sip of his wine. "You are certainly more interesting to talk to than most others here tonight. But be careful with whom you share your admiration for this man. Some are more sensitive than I. The war against the Gauls is costing the Empire dearly, both in men and funds."

I nodded my understanding as I reached toward a bowl piled high with ripe peaches. I offered one to Flavius, which he accepted with a smile. *Good*, I thought, *we're friends again, just don't express your opinions too readily.* I bit into the peach. It was a little too ripe and the juice ran down my chin onto my tunic. With a mild curse and a laugh I cupped my hand under my chin. Flavius picked up a napkin, and coming closer on the couch, dabbed at my chin, all the while smiling into my eyes.

He really is a handsome man, I thought, and wondered if I could go as far as to bed him to get what I wanted. Why not? I did it with Petronius—but then, he was a friend, and I wanted nothing more from him than comfort and affection. With Flavius, it would be different. If I could ensnare his affections, it would be in order to exact a favor from him—a favor that might bring me closer to finding Callistus. However, from the look in the Tribune's eyes I had the feeling that if I did bed him, I'd be the one bestowing the favor!

"May I see you to your home, when it's time to leave?" he asked, with a final dab at my chin. "I have a litter outside."

"If it's no trouble."

"It will be my pleasure." He stood, smoothing the front of his tunic. With his crotch at my eye level, I was able to see quite plainly that the Tribune was aroused. "Now, I think we'd better mingle a little with the other guests."

Papni hovered about me, trying to find out just how successful his attempt at matchmaking had been. Of course, I wasn't about to tell him of the effect I'd had on Flavius, but I did mention that he had offered me a ride home in his litter.

"Perfect," he crowed, clapping his hands together with delight. "Ask him in for some wine. He'll be falling over his feet with the anticipation of being alone with you."

I chuckled. "You have a wonderful opinion of my allure, my friend. I think the Tribune is just lonely, away from his regiment and his friends."

"Hmm, we'll see—and don't forget, if something wondrous happens, you owe it all to my machinations." He giggled, then added. "Well, perhaps a little also to your allure!"

I smiled, not wanting to dampen his spirits by telling him that "something wondrous happening" would have to mean Callistus suddenly appearing in the room, ready to take me in his arms, and swearing to never leave me again.

As we bade him goodnight, Papni gave me a theatrical wink, rubbing his hands together with apparent glee that his ploy of putting Flavius and I together had worked extremely well—in his mind anyway.

"How do you know Venel Papni?" Flavius asked me, as the bearers of his covered litter plodded along the road. "He doesn't strike me as the sort of man you would include in your circle of friends."

"He was… a friend of my father's," I said, lying just a little. Papni and my father had been business acquaintances, not friends, but this was a better story than the truth. The brave Tribune might have been just a little shocked to learn the reality of my relationship with the Etruscan merchant. "When my father died, he was very conciliatory, and I appreciated his concern."

Flavius moved closer and put his arm around my shoulders. I did not move away. "He is a great admirer of yours," he said, his free hand touching my thigh. "Before you arrived, he had regaled me with your many virtues and your intelligence."

I laughed lightly. "He had? Papni is extravagant in everything, including his praise."

"Perhaps." He began stroking my thigh, and his lips touched the corner of my eye, lingering there for a moment before he tilted my face to his and kissed me full on the mouth. It was a nice kiss. The fact that I felt nothing from it was not his fault, but mine. I put my hand behind his head and pulled him in, pressing my lips to his. The litter lurched suddenly as one of the bearers stumbled on the cobbled street. Flavius winced as I inadvertently bit his lip.

"Oh, sorry," I whispered, watching him dab at his lip with his forefinger. "Here," I leaned forward and licked the blood away. He stared into my eyes for a long moment before grabbing me in his arms and crushing my mouth with his. As his tongue slipped between my parted lips, there was no denying the eroticism between us at that moment. Despite myself, I felt a deep carnal pleasure in the feel of his hard body beneath my hands.

We broke apart as the litter came to a halt outside my house. "Would you care for a cup of wine before you leave?" I asked, as instructed by Papni.

"Unfortunately, I'm expected by General Galbus and his wife for a late supper. I'm staying with them while here in Capua. But let me walk you to your door."

I have to admit to a vague feeling of disappointment at his refusal, but thought it was just as well. The kiss we had shared had awakened a need in me—and not one I was prepared to readily accept. At my door, Flavius pulled me into his arms and kissed me again.

"Are you free tomorrow afternoon?" he asked, his lips on my ear.

"Yes. I have some lessons to prepare, but they can wait."

"Good. I'll bring my horse, and we can take a ride into the countryside. Would you like that?"

"Yes…"

He kissed me again. "At two then," he said, before striding off, leaving me to fumble with the lock.

I walked through the darkened room, my mind blurred by all that had just taken place. I had told Rufus not to wait up for me, and I was glad of the solitude of the moment. I found some wine in an earthenware pitcher and poured myself a cup, then took it to my room, where I decided I needed to think things through more clearly. Just what was I doing? I asked myself as I sank into the comfort of my bed, propping my head up on several pillows and taking a long slow pull on my wine. Flavius was attractive, and there was no doubt I had felt the tug of desire when he had kissed me that second time in the litter. But I could not let carnal need stand in the way of what I really wanted from him.

The Tribune was the very man who could aid me with the plan that now spun in my mind—a plan as yet still vague and perhaps foolhardy. But when had that ever stopped me in my purpose? My friends all considered me slightly mad, all this would do when first they heard of it was convince them that they had been correct all along.

When next I saw Flavius, I would be honest. Not about Callistus, but about what I needed him to do for me. Then I would see if his affection for me extended to what I would ask.

CHAPTER III

Flavius was at my door promptly at two the following afternoon. He had shed his uniform in favor of a light blue tunic. A clever choice, I thought, seeing how it emphasized the blue of his eyes. I greeted him with a smile as Rufus ushered him in, and asked if he wished anything to drink—cold water, some honey wine...

"No, the General's wife prepared a very fine lunch." He rubbed his flat stomach in appreciation. "Anything more and I might burst!" He looked around the room as he spoke. "A fine home, Lucius. Your father must have left you in good stead."

Rufus and I exchanged small smiles at that remark. Rufus knew of the crushing debts my father had left behind, but now was not the time to correct the Tribune.

"Yes," I said. "And now that my mother has wed again, I find myself free to spread into every room. Poor Rufus has more work now then when we had a full household."

Flavius smile politely at my weak humor, but seemed anxious to get going. "Do you ride?" he asked. "I brought a second horse for you."

I nodded. "I had a horse of my own once," I said, thinking of Belenus, the steed Callistus had given me to return home from his encampment.

"Wonderful, so let's go, shall we? It's a beautiful day." I followed him as he strode outside to the gate where he had tied up the horses. "The bay is yours," said, indicating the beautiful creature that regarded me from dark brown eyes. Its black mane and tail were in perfect contrast to the coppery brown body.

"He's a beauty," I murmured, stroking his muzzle. "What is he called?"

"I'm afraid I don't know."

"But a horse must have a name. Just for today, I will call you Belenus," I said, blowing gently into the bay's nostrils.

"Belenus... a strange name."

"It's the name of a Gallic god. It means 'bright one.'"

Flavius handed me the reins. "You seem to know a lot about the Gauls," he remarked, mounting his black steed.

"I am a teacher." I heaved myself up into the bay's saddle. "It's my duty to know these things."

"Of course." He said no more as we made our way down the narrow street that would eventually take us to the open roads and fields beyond. He was right, it was a beautiful day; the sun warming my face and bare arms.

"How long do you plan on staying in Capua?" I asked.

"Only for three more days. Then I join General Mateus in Cisalpine Gaul. There is unrest there, border raids and the like."

Three days. I was going to have to act quickly. We had reached the open country road and he spurred his horse into a brisk canter. I followed, staying just a head behind him. He turned in his saddle and grinned at me.

"Race?" he yelled.

I nodded, spurring "Belenus" forward and passing him at a gallop. I heard his shout of laughter behind me, then glancing back I saw him close behind, urging his horse to close the gap between us. I let Belenus have free rein, and the bay increased his speed, widening the lead we had over Flavius and his mount.

Of course, I was going to let him win. I just didn't want it to look too easy.

I headed toward a wooded area, gently easing back, slowing our pace, being careful not to make it look too obvious. He passed us with a shout of glee, stopping short of the trees, then turned, his horse rearing up in apparent triumph. I acknowledged his prowess with a wave as we cantered up to where he waited, beaming broadly.

"Did you just let me win?"

"Of course not," I replied, dismounting. "You are obviously the better rider."

He leapt from the saddle and looped the reins over the branch of a tree. He approached me, shaking his head in disbelief.

"Lucius Tullius..." He pulled me into his arms. "I do believe you are something of a liar."

I chuckled and gave in to his embrace. "Sir, I must take offense at those words..."

His lips found mine in a bruising kiss, bringing an end to words, and the beginning of an emotional turmoil to my mind. I tried telling myself this was merely a means to an end, that the fire he was starting in my loins meant nothing, that the feel of his hard arousal pressing against my thigh was of no consequence, and that at any moment I could disengage myself from his arms and walk away from him without a backward glance. I wasn't really going to let him lead me into the woods, lie with me on the leafy ground, kiss my brow, my eyes, my lips, while his hands found their way under my tunic to my bare skin. Nor was I going to allow him to caress each and every part of my body, until my need for his touch became so apparent that I returned all of this to him with a fervor I found I could not control. Of course I was not...

I helped him pull his tunic over his head. My hands roamed over his muscular back, feeling the strength overlain with smooth and supple skin. He lowered his face to mine, his lips brushing over mine, then taking them in a rough, demanding kiss. His tongue slid into my mouth, and he let out a long, breathy moan. His breath quickened as I reached between his legs and found his stiff, hard cock. I broke off our kiss long enough to spit into my hand and wrap it around the throbbing flesh while his hips moved over me, and his cock slid in and out of my grasp. Running my thumb over the slit, I smeared the copious juice that spilled from it over the length of the shaft.

I wound my legs around his waist and raised my hips, guiding his erection to my opening. He groaned as he pushed himself into my hot core. I braced myself against the pain that came before the ecstasy, wrapping my arms and legs around his torso, holding him a willing prisoner as he thrust deep inside me. I tried not to compare what was happening with anything that had gone before, and indeed, Flavius was doing a sterling job of fucking me. As he pounded into me, I cupped my hands around his buttocks, pulling him in ever deeper. I let a finger stray into his anus, pushing past his resistance, stroking his prostate. His expression became one of pure rapture. His body arched in ecstasy, he gave a great shout as his orgasm overtook him and he exploded inside me, searing my intestines with his hot semen. I held him in my arms as he collapsed over me, his face pressed to my neck, until his breathing returned to normal.

After a few moments he raised his head to look at me. "You did not find release."

"Your pleasure was also mine," I said.

"Are you sure?"

"Yes, I am sure."

He gazed into my dark eyes for a long moment as if trying to read what lay behind them. Then he rested his head on my shoulder with a sigh.

"It was wonderful for me. You are a beautiful man, Lucius." His hand caressed my chest, then he pulled me in close to his body. "I would take you with me on my next campaign, if it were possible."

I stiffened with surprise. Could it be this easy? "That's strange," I said quietly. "It has been on my mind to rejoin the army. More so, since I met you."

This time it was his turn to be surprised. "You were thinking on this?"

"Only if I could serve with your legion, of course."

"Are your serious, Lucius? It would mean a tremendous change in your life."

"I was a soldier before," I told him. "When I was but twenty."

"Did you see any action?"

"Some, but it was mostly on patrol, keeping the peace."

He sat up, grinning at me. "Then come with me to Rome and enlist. I'll make sure you are garrisoned near me, and a recruit for my next campaign."

My heart beat the faster at his words. He had already told me he was to march to Cisalpine Gaul, and that he had seen a warrior, whom I was sure was Callistus, on the battlefield. If I could only be that much closer to Callistus, I would work on the rest of my plan later. As mad as it sounded, this is what I had been waiting for. While I had been responsible for my mother and sisters' welfare, I had bided my time, but now, as Petronius had said, I was free to do whatever my heart desired.

I looked at the Tribune's happy smile and felt a twinge of shame at using him to further my own self-interest. If he had any idea that the man I longed to follow was not him, but an enemy of the Empire, that smile would slip from his face in an instant. The carnal pleasure I had just brought him would soon be forgotten and replaced with anger, and no doubt hatred for me. It would be up to me to ensure he never found out.

✖ ✖ ✖ ✖ ✖

The reaction of my friends and family on hearing my decision to rejoin the army was as I expected. Tears, and pleas to change my mind, from my mother and sisters, anger from Petronius, disbelief from Turio and Dido, and a wretched lecture from my employer.

"What in the name of all the gods are you thinking, Lucius?" he bellowed at me in the confines of his private room at the school. "You of all people, giving up a fine career, that might even lead you to politics, to follow the Roman army into the land of the barbarians. You, who are not even Roman, but a citizen of Capua. What has brought you to this madness?"

Of course, I could not tell him the real reasons, so I merely mumbled some nonsense about wanting excitement in my life before I became too old to act upon it. His exclamation of disgust echoed in my ears as I took my leave of him—and the school.

Petronius was harder to deal with. We had been friends and occasional lovers for years. I knew I was going to miss him more than any of my other friends, but even his angry tears could not dissuade me. I tried my best to calm him, even made love to him as he buried his wet face against my neck and held me as if he would never let me go. But, even after, he would not be appeased, and I was forced to leave him in my bed and sit alone in the darkened courtyard. When he eventually composed himself and started to bid me a cold farewell, I took his hand and begged him to forgive me.

"I know why you're doing this," he said, his eyes still red from his tears. "You think you're going to find that barbarian. You're mad, Lucius, quite mad. Even if you did find him, what use for you would he have? Three years since you last saw him. If he's still alive he's most likely wed, and a father—if he wasn't already before you met him. Do you really think he will have any need for you in his life now? He's a *barbarian*, Lucius. An uncivilized lout who would as soon put a knife in you as—"

"Stop it!" I leaped to my feet, my face hot with anger. Petronius took a startled step back from me. "Don't talk of him like that," I seethed. "You know nothing of him. You would judge a man you've never met, nor spoken to? In my mind he is everything I ever wanted, and more. It was we, the so-called civilized ones, who enslaved him and forced him into the arena. In his own land he is a man of worth—a leader and a champion of his people. Do not denigrate him in front of me ever again!"

Petronius gave me a long, hard look, then he turned on his heel and strode from the courtyard, slamming the gate behind him.

"*Petronius*," I murmured, sinking back down onto the stone bench. "Why could *you* not understand?"

But, of course, I had to be honest with myself. Yes, I was joining the Roman army with only one thought in mind—a means to find Callistus. Madness yes, but a madness created by a need that never diminished, no matter how many years went by. Nothing, no one, was more important to me. This might be the most foolish thing I had ever done, but if I did not do it, I would live with the regret of chances lost for the rest of my life. If it all came to naught, if I died in the attempt, at least I could say I tried.

CHAPTER IV

The clanking of metal and heavy boots awakened me. I sat up in my narrow cot, rubbing my eyes and looking around me at the rows of similar cots, some empty, some with men still slumbering after the grueling day before of training and marching.

What in Hades had I got myself into, I wondered, not for the first time. Two months of hell, and I still did not know just where I was going. Nor had I seen Flavius. That irked me beyond all else.

"Come with me to Rome," he'd said, and I, thinking that he would be of some help, had foolishly complied. It would have been just the same if I'd made my own way, for on our arrival he turned me over to the enlisting officers, and that was the last I saw of him. For over a month I had marched until I thought my feet would fall off; I had trained with sword, lance and axe until I feared my arms would fall off, and still the relentless punishment to my body and spirit went on—and on.

Still, I had to admit that even though my mind was bored into numbness by the repetitious routines, my body had already slimmed and hardened from the hard work. If only they would tell us we were to move out on campaign. Any campaign, but hopefully to Gaul.

Most nights when I fell onto my bed I was too tired to think of anything but sleep, yet so many times since I'd been in these barracks I had dreamed of Callistus. Sometimes, the dreams were so intense that I would awaken, certain that I had been moaning, or muttering aloud of my longing for the man who haunted my sleeping hours. So far, to my relief, none of my fellow soldiers had mentioned any strange nighttime behavior from me. Most of them slept like the dead anyway.

"Private Tullius..." I jerked my head toward the barracks door as my name was called out.

"Here," I shouted.

"Tribune Sedonius wants to see you in his quarters. Make haste, he's in a hurry."

Is he now? I thought, struggling out from under the blanket. Almost eight weeks, and he's finally deigned to acknowledge my presence—and he's in a hurry. Even after all this time, I still had a hard time thinking of Flavius as my superior officer. To me, he was the man I'd let fuck me. Not the proper attitude, I suppose, but as I'd yet to see him in his leadership role, I felt I could be less than charitable. Nevertheless, I hurried through my ablutions and got my uniform on in record time, despite the clumsiness of the clasps and buckles.

I eventually found my way to his quarters after a couple of wrong turns, and announced myself to the duty guard posted outside. Flavius greeted me with an ebullient smile and, as we were alone, a quick embrace.

"Good news, Lucius," he said, beaming at me. "In fact, the best kind of news, for you."

"For me?"

"Yes. General Mateus has need of a secretary. Apparently, the man who has served him for the last four years has been taken ill—severe pains in his abdomen. I recommended you for the post, citing your scholarship and teaching ability."

"Why, that is very generous of you, Flavius... I mean, Tribune Sedonius. Thank you, very much."

He smiled. "When we're alone, Lucius, you may call me Flavius. Now, the General leaves today..."

My heart lurched in my chest. "For Gaul?"

"No, there is a deal of trouble in Iberia. Some of the tribes there are rebelling again, so the General has been given orders to subdue them as quickly as possible."

I stared at him, trying to hide my disbelief and disappointment. Iberia was very much in the wrong direction, so even though my standing in the ranks may have just improved, I was moving that much farther away from my goal of finding Callistus. Of course, I realized that there was nothing I could do about it at that moment. To refuse to accompany the General on his campaign was tantamount to desertion and would result in a death sentence, or at the very least a flogging that would most likely kill me.

"You seem reticent, Lucius," Flavius said, his tone peevish. "Are you not pleased with this piece of good fortune?"

I smiled quickly. It would not do to upset Flavius. I might just need him again. "Indeed, I am pleased, Flavius, and again I thank you. Are you joining the General on his campaign?"

"No, my orders haven't changed. I leave for Cisalpine Gaul tomorrow morning." He touched my cheek with his fingertips. "I am afraid that, as much as I would like to have your company one last time before I leave, I have official duties to attend to this evening."

I nodded my understanding. "Then we must wait to savor those delights another day," I said smoothly. He pulled me into his arms and kissed me. He was rough and demanding. I could sense his need, and his frustration, and for a moment I thought he meant to take me right there in his quarters. Then his disciplined mind took over and he thrust me away with a sigh of what I took to be regret.

"My apologies, Lucius, but I must go."

"Of course," I said, masking my relief at his change of mood. "Should I introduce myself to the General right away?"

"I'll take you there now." He picked up his helmet and led me from the room. We walked in silence to the General's quarters, where he informed the guard that he had brought General Mateus' new secretary and I should be admitted at once.

Mateus was an imposing figure of a man. Tall, as tall as Callistus I judged him to be, and with a head of close-cropped white hair. He was lean, his face lined and weather-beaten from his constant campaigning in foreign lands. He looked me over carefully after Flavius had introduced me.

"You're young for this, aren't you?" he stated, rather than asked.

"I'm twenty-six, sir," I replied, hoping he would dismiss me and I could join Flavius on his march to Gaul.

"You look younger, but I daresay you'll do," he muttered. "You'll attend all my strategy meetings with my officers, and transcribe all that is said, leaving nothing out. Understand?"

"Yes, sir."

Flavius saluted him. "I'll take my leave then, General, if you have nothing more for me…"

Mateus regarded him coolly for a second or two, then nodded. "The gods be with you, Tribune Sedonius. You'll need them by your side where you're going. Those savages seem to grow stronger with each passing day." He gave a cursory salute, then turned to look at me again as Flavius left. "You can start by writing a letter to my wife. There's parchment and stylus on the desk there."

I hastened to do as he bid, and for the next hour or so was regaled with the boring details of his personal life as Mateus droned on and on about how devastated he was not to see his dear wife before leaving on his campaign to Iberia. I wondered, as I wrote, if she would feel a sense of loss, or great relief, when she received his missive. I was already beginning to feel claustrophobic in his presence, and suddenly was not at all looking forward to attending to him in my secretarial duties. Ah well, I thought as I scraped away laboriously, such are the vagaries of life.

✖ ✖ ✖ ✖ ✖

We left for Iberia two days later. Two days in which I was almost constantly in the General's company, scribbling one detailed strategy after another for the subduing of the rebels. With so many alternative plans, I imagined his officers running around in mass confusion as they tried to remember just which one he had chosen to follow.

Even as we marched, I was not spared his outpouring of ideas. The good news was I had been given a horse for the journey to Iberia, the bad news was I had to ride alongside Mateus, listening and writing down his endless theories on how best to defeat, then contain the rebel armies. His endless stream of conversation, mostly uttered as though he were talking to himself, finally became an annoying babble to my ears. Nevertheless, diligent secretary that I was, I transcribed each and every word of his tedious rhetoric. Perhaps, one day, someone might mange to make some sense of it, but from what I overheard among the officers complaining, it would not be any of them.

We were attacked on the road to Navania—an ambush, taking us entirely by surprise, and with deadly results. Many of our soldiers were either killed or badly wounded, necessitating a field hospital to be erected. Mateus, thoroughly humiliated and enraged by the rebels' audacity, took a large force and set off into the hills in pursuit of the attackers, taking me along to record the Iberian's defeat and punishment. Only that was not the way it happened.

A day later, much to Mateus' chagrin, his scouts reported there was no sign of the rebels. His officers advised returning to the main road to Navania, and a continuance of the march to the city. Mateus would hear none of it.

"What? Let them think they are better than the Roman Army?" he bellowed, his face red with rage. "This is not how the Empire was founded. We do not accept defeat. We will find them and annihilate them. I will accept nothing less."

And so we pushed on into the hills—wild, desolate country that held many traps for the unwary. Hidden ravines, narrow passes that forced us to march single file—easy pickings for rebel archers. Yet strangely we were not attacked—until we found ourselves on open ground, sitting targets for the rebels who appeared as if from nowhere, screaming down upon us, hacking and slashing with devastating force. Before Mateus could give any order, he was struck from his horse by a spear imbedded in his chest. I watched with horror as he toppled from his saddle, a look of total surprise on his face. He lay on his back, clutching at the long wooden shaft in a futile attempt to pull it free. I leaped from my horse and knelt by his side, but then his head lolled to one side and a great gout of blood spilled from his mouth.

I unsheathed my sword and stood by the other soldiers as the rebels slammed into us. I came face to face with an ugly, swarthy-faced half-naked devil who leered at me, showing blackened teeth set in a wicked smile. I managed to parry his first blow to my head, but then his sheer size made me stagger back, tripping over a body behind me. He loomed over me, his axe raised to strike, when suddenly his head just disappeared, lopped from his shoulders by the swing of an infantryman's *gladius*. He went down in a welter of blood that splashed over me, the stench of gore making me want to retch. Except there was no time for that. The soldier who had saved my life was now himself being attacked by two fiends, shrieking war cries and battering at his shield with clubs. I sprang to his aid, slashing at one rebel with my sword and wounding him. He screamed, turning on me with an expression that almost froze my blood. Despite his wound, he launched himself at me, and we crashed to the stony ground, he pounding at my head with his fists and screaming at the top of his voice. Fortunately, I still had my sword. I thrust it between his ribs, and twisted. He gave a great gurgling cry and fell off me, rolling away, allowing me to jump to my feet. My fellow soldier was not so lucky. He lay dead, a rebel dagger in his chest.

I looked around me, and to my dismay found I was one of only a few soldiers still standing. We were completely surrounded by rebels, who now signaled for our surrender. Several soldiers threw down their swords, and I, seeing no point in trying to fight them all single handedly, followed suit. I expected a swift death, but instead we were rounded up, pushed, beaten and spat upon by our captors, then marched off toward their encampment. Well, I thought, as I trudged along, growling at those who kicked and shoved me, this is not what I had planned at all. Only two months in the army and I was already a prisoner, and most likely condemned to die some awful death at the hands of these rogues. It seemed the gods were not going to make my quest to find Callistus an easy one.

The rebel village was alive with the sounds of victory as my fellow prisoners and I were marched into what must have been their equivalent of a forum, a meeting place where we were displayed like cattle while the crowds jeered and threw stones and horse dung at us. Again, I prepared myself to die, my only regret being my failure to find Callistus before I coughed up my last breath.

A large man, his face behind his beard lined and swarthy, stepped forward and regarded us with a disdainful eye. I glared back at him, determined not to be cowed by these people. They were rebels after all—enemies of the Empire. He caught my eyes and grinned, showing yellow teeth. I shuddered, thinking for the moment that he meant to take me for his own pleasure. *Let me die*, I thought, but then, if it meant I might live and yet find Callistus… He reached for me. Grabbing me roughly, he turned me around, then ripped my tunic from my body. I stood there, naked and humiliated, while he barked some words at the crowd.

To my horror, I realized I was being auctioned—as a slave. A woman, licking her lips as her eyes traveled the length of my body, raised her hand. The man barked some unintelligible words, and then a man farther back in the crowd raised his hand. For a time, it went back and forth, first the woman would raise her hand, then the man, and then the woman again, and so forth. Eventually, her face turning sour, she gave up and directed her eyes to the young soldier next to me. I was cuffed on the back of the head, then led away to my owner, a tall, older man, dressed in decent enough clothing. He said something to the auctioneer, who scowled then handed him my tunic, which in turn he gave to me. Gratefully, I slipped it over my head. I was not ashamed of my body, and had been naked many times in front of other people, but there was just something degrading about it now.

I followed the man away from the unfriendly crowd, trotting at his heels as he pulled on the rope that bound my wrists. He walked with a certain stiffness I had seen in older men, or those with back injuries. *What in Hades was to be my fate now?* Was I to be the man's catamite, his slave for pleasure just as Venel Papni's servants were? Was I to be passed around his friends for an evening's diversion? Of all the things that I thought might happen to me in my lifetime, never did I envision this. A prisoner, perhaps—death by sword or spear thrust even—but this, this humiliation was more than I could bear.

We passed through a large arched gateway, into a pleasant enough garden filled with the aroma of flowers and herbs. The house, its design crude by Capuan standards, was nevertheless large, and its white walls gleaming in the sunlight gave off a feeling of solidity and permanence. A woman appeared in the doorway, along with two small children, who stared at me with big eyes from solemn faces.

The man unbound my hands. "Can I trust you not to run?" he said in fair Latin. "If so, there will be no need to bind your feet."

I nodded. Where, after all, would I run to? The army I had marched with was destroyed. I had not the slightest notion as to where I was. My best plan was to wait for the Romans to send another army to punish this insurrection. I was certain that this defeat, and the death of General Mateus, would be enough to incense the Senate into decisive action. Looking around, I did not sense any immediate danger to my person. The man, his wife and children, were a picture of domesticity. Perhaps this would not turn out as badly as I had at first feared.

"I will not run," I said, answering his question. "What are to be my duties here?"

"Our servants joined the fight against the Romans," he replied. "You will replace them until they return, if they ever do. There is a lot of work needed here, in the garden alone. I have not the back for it anymore, and my wife, Selena, has the children to tend." He looked at me without animosity. "What is your name?"

"Lucius... and do I simply call you Master?"

He chuckled. "My name is Canto." He smiled as his wife and children drew near. "My wife, Selena, and my two daughters, Destina and Fortuna."

"Destiny and Fortune," I murmured as the little ones stared up at me. "Providential names. I hope their lives proved to be as fortunate."

"What were you in private life?" Selena asked.

I smiled wryly. "A teacher, Mistress. Though it would appear not a very wise one."

"Perhaps you could tutor my daughters," Canto said. "I would like for them to learn Latin. It might prove very useful to them one day."

I could scarcely believe my luck. How many prisoners of war have ever found themselves in the midst of such a friendly and docile family? Few, I would imagine, if any. Perhaps the gods had decided to smile on me again, and give me the strength to one day continue my quest to find Callistus. In the meantime, until all things changed once again, I would tend Canto's garden and instruct his children in Latin and their lessons. Who but the gods knew how long my stay here would last? I smiled at the little ones as they took my hands in their tiny ones and led me into the house. My stomach growled at the aroma of vegetables and herbs simmering in the pot over the fire. Prisoner's fare, it seemed, was to be better by far than that of a soldier.

CHAPTER V

CISALPINE GAUL, SIX MONTHS LATER

CALLISTUS

An early morning gray light was stealing into my tent as I awoke from yet another restless sleep. How, I wondered perhaps for the thousandth time, how after almost four years could the memory of one man still haunt my dreams at night, and my thoughts by day? Had he possessed some magical power that kept me still pining for his caresses after all this time? True, in his bewitching brown eyes I had been lost several times, finding myself letting him do things to me no other man had—or had since. Even during my marriage to Edina, I had not felt the same passion or longing with which he had imbued me—or cursed me, as it sometimes felt. For what was the point of all this longing for a man I would never see again.

Lucius...

"I will return to you one day," I had promised him, and at the time I had meant those words. I'd had a vision of myself, sitting astride brave Belenus, cantering up to his home, gathering him in my arms, and riding off with him to a secure and blessed future. What folly I now knew this to be. There could be no future for Lucius and I. Even though I was now a widower, my wife having died in one of the endless conflicts between my people and the Roman armies, the possibility of ever seeing him again was something I could not, in reality, foresee.

"Prince Callistus..." My thoughts were brought to an abrupt end by the voice outside my tent, of Castes, one of my captains.

"Come in, Castes," I groaned, rolling off my cot. I stood and stretched as he entered, then as I sensed his eyes roaming over my naked body, I hastily covered myself. I had been aware of his admiration for me for some time, but I would never take a lover from within the ranks. Such things lead to jealousy and trouble among the other men. Besides, because of Lucius, I had been spoiled for any other man.

"You have news?" I asked, pulling my leggings over my thighs.

His eyes finally met mine and he nodded. "Romans, two cohorts a few miles south of here. They are burning everything in their path."

"Is there anything left to burn?" I shook my head as if to answer my own rhetorical question. Since the end of the servile war under Spartacus, I had fought the Romans unceasingly, sometimes with success, sometimes with defeat, but always with vicious plundering and burning of homes and countryside. Just how much more of this pestilence could our world survive?

"Alert the men," I said. "We'll march in an hour."

"Yes, my prince. I'll have one of the men bring you bread and wine."

I sighed as he left. It never ceased to amaze me that my men stayed so loyal to me. We'd had successes, yes, but the cost had, at times, been appalling and the hardships they'd had to bear, crushing. Still, as they said, what was the alternative? Slavery and servitude under the Roman heel, and there was not one man worth his mettle who could endure that humiliation. Freedom, or death with honor, was what they craved, and in me I think they saw that same resolve. Those reasons alone kept them by my side, for the spoils of war were now few and far between.

I thanked the soldier who brought me a hunk of bread and a cup of watered wine. Before putting on my armor, I sat staring into the blood red liquid, and once more my thoughts turned to Lucius. "Where are you?" I wondered aloud. "How has your life been since I last saw you?" Had he taken a lover, or married, like myself? A marriage forced upon me by the wishes of the people. A marriage that was to produce a son and heir, but had proved fruitless. Perhaps by now, Lucius was a father. I smiled at the thought. He'd be a good father.

For what I remembered most about him was not the powerful passions that had raged between us, wonderful and unforgettable though they were, but the sweetness of his kisses after we had made love, the soft whisper of his lips on mine as he told me of his love for me. How I longed for those times again. Brief as it had been, it was the happiest time of my life.

✻ ✻ ✻ ✻ ✻

The Romans, as always, had made good time since the news of their approach had been brought to me. Despite my hatred for them, I could not quite suppress my admiration for the way they conducted their campaigns. If only I could instill this same discipline into the separate tribes—if I could have them all under one standard, just once, I was sure we could chase the Roman legions from our homeland, and never see them again. But our weakness was in our pride, and in our loyalty divided between too many leaders. Time and again I had tried to talk them into forming one vast, unbeatable army, even showing myself willing to step down as commander, if we could elect a leader we could all follow. But my pleas had fallen on deaf ears. The glory of victory was not something our kings wanted to share.

Today, because of the preparations I had made for just such an action from the enemy, I knew we would prevail. Outnumbered we might be, but there many ways to win a battle, and one of them is surprise. Of course, the Romans would be on the alert for any sign of an ambush, but the sheer size of their armies made them vulnerable to sneak attacks, such as the one we would now employ. My men, hidden from sight by the rough and wooded terrain, skirted both sides of the enemy's flanks. At a signal from Thalanius, my second-in-command, the archers would begin a deadly fire that would throw the Romans into confusion. That would be my signal to attack.

I reined in my horse and watched from my vantage point as Thalanius readied his archers. The steady tread of the marching soldiers was suddenly disrupted as the first wave of arrows descended upon the Romans ranks, bringing instant death to many of the soldiers. As the screams of the wounded rent the air, I gave the order to attack and led my cavalry and foot soldiers in a devastating charge that took out the main body of infantrymen in less than five minutes. But the Romans were not finished, far from it. Their commanders, shouting orders, had them regroup and fight back, driving my foot soldiers back by sheer force of numbers. I spurred my mount on, yelling for my cavalry to follow in a second charge on the Roman ranks. This time, they broke and ran, leaving their officers defenseless, most of whom were quickly cut down.

The surviving officers were brought before me, scowling their defiance with the usual Roman arrogance. One of them, however, met my eyes with a quizzical expression. A tribune; young, handsome, with an air of intelligence and breeding.

"Your name?" I asked, directing my attention to him.

"Tribune Flavius Sedonius."

"I am Prince Callistus of the Helvetii. You and your men are invading the territory I defend. Why?"

"We are under orders to bring this rebellion to an end."

"Rebellion..." I smiled wryly. "You speak as though we were your subjects, Tribune Sedonius. I have signed no document that allows Rome to govern my country. You are invaders, we the defenders. And as of this moment, you are the vanquished."

Sedonius bowed his head slightly in agreement. "You mean to ransom us?"

"Are you of some worth, Tribune?"

He smiled. "There are some who might consider me of some value. My mother, for instance."

"Ah, your mother still lives. You are a fortunate man, Tribune. Most of my men here have seen both their parents die of starvation, or on the point of Roman swords. Their wives and children too. Victims of a foe that cares little for human life in its quest for conquest and power. So, tell me honestly, Tribune, if you were me, and had their murderers in your grasp, would you ransom them, or put them to the sword?"

Before he could answer, one of the other officers yelled, "Barbarian! You would dare defy the might of Rome? You will be dragged through its streets, shackled to our chariots, lashed until you fall to your knees in obeisance to Rome's power!" A chorus of assent rose from the throats of his companions, while my men, who, although they could not all understand the Roman's words, could at least recognize his tone as a threat to me, and raised their weapons in anger.

I held up my hand to calm them. "Your words are meaningless here," I told the officer. "You are my prisoners, and as such your lives are very much in my hands. Whether you live or die is my decision—but know this, your deaths will be clean and quick. There is no satisfaction for me in watching men suffer needlessly. The Roman habit of mindless torture and slaughter is not our way. We fight to defend our land, and we will to the bitter end. There will be no Roman conquest of Gaul, while I am alive. Now..." I signaled my men. "Take them away until the morrow, when we will decide their fate. Tribune Sedonius, you will stay here with me."

He approached me slowly, his eyes wary. "When you asked me what I would do if my parents' murderers were in my grasp, was that merely a rhetorical question, or were you interested in my answer?"

I chuckled. "I can guess what your answer would be, Tribune."

"Can you?" His clear blue eyes gleamed with intensity as he spoke. "You think I would say, 'ransom them rather than execute them'? That would be the easy way out, of course, and the answer you expect. But, like you, I would rather see my parents' murderers pay for their crimes with their lives. You are right, I am fortunate in that I still have a mother safe and sound at home. It may cause you to doubt my sincerity when I say I am sorry for your loss, nevertheless I will say it—I am sorry."

"A Roman with a conscience, now that's a rarity," I said, with mock admiration.

He nodded. "I understand your cynicism."

"Do you also understand what I must do?"

"Of course. This is war, and we are the enemy." Sedonius paused for a moment, then asked quietly. "Do you intend to execute us? If so, I would like to send a letter to my family, and another—to a friend."

I shook my head. "I am not one for mindless slaughter. You and your fellow officers will be released. I think the shame of the defeat you suffered here might prove to be a worse punishment when you return to Rome, and have to face the wrath of the Senate."

He gave a rueful smile. "You may be right in that."

"However, I will keep some prisoners to be held for ransom." I shrugged slightly as I stood. "We are not above exacting money from the Roman coffers. If Rome pays the ransom, the men will be set free to return home. If not, they will be executed."

"Then I would stay with those of my men you hold," he said.

"Why?"

"Because they have a better chance of being ransomed if an officer is among them. Besides, I have some connections in Rome—rich connections. If it's money you want, I can get it for you."

"Big words, Tribune," I said, raising an eyebrow. "Be careful that you don't have to eat them."

"I won't."

His smile held that Roman arrogance I so detested, yet I could not fault his bravery in offering to stay with his men— something I would not have thought him capable of.

He cleared his throat. "May I ask you a question?"

"Ask."

"Does the name Lucius Tullius mean anything to you?"

I leveled a steady gaze at him, trying to hide my surprise at his question. Lucius? What did he know of him? "Lucius Tullius," I said slowly. "Yes, I remember him. He tried to arbitrate between Spartacus and Lentullus Batiatus, the *ludo* owner. Why do you ask?"

"I sensed he has a great admiration for you. When I mentioned that I had met the Gauls in battle led by someone with your appearance, he became quite excited, wanting to know more of you, or rather, the warrior who looked like you. He said..."

"A warrior who looked like me?" I interrupted him.

"Well, of course, it was you. I would recognize you anywhere." His eyes regarded me with frank admiration. "I can see why Lucius would want to know more of your whereabouts, if you had survived the wars. That kind of thing..."

"And this Lucius," I said, in an offhanded manner. "Where is he now?"

Sedonius smiled. No doubt he could see through my seeming indifference. "He joined the army. Now when I think of it, it may have been just so he might find you. Unfortunately, he was recruited by General Mateus to be his secretary on his campaign to subdue the rebels in Iberia."

I felt a sickening in the pit of my stomach. Lucius, in the Roman army! Regardless of the fact he would not be on the front line, campaigning against rebel armies fighting for their survival would bring him close to danger at almost every turn. I tried to erase the vision that had flashed before my eyes, of him fighting for his life against the Iberian hordes. What, in the name of all the gods, had possessed him to do such a lunatic thing? Of course, I knew the answer, and my heart quickened in my chest at the realization that his love for me had not faded with the passage of time, just as mine for him had remained as constant as the stars in their heavens.

"Prince Callistus?" Sedonius was regarding me with a mixture of amusement and concern on his face. My prolonged silence had obviously aroused his curiosity as to the exact nature of my relationship with Lucius. It would not do for him to know any more than what he had guessed at. Lucius might suffer because of this man's prying.

"Why would you say he joined the army to look for me?" I asked, anger coloring my voice. "I am his enemy, as well as yours. The boy was an envoy, who meant well, but failed in his mission to bring compromise between Batiatus and the gladiators. That is all."

He bowed in deference to my words. "My apologies Prince, I'm afraid young Lucius made it seem more than it really was."

"Indeed," I said, turning from him. "You may join your fellow officers, Tribune. Tomorrow, I will decide who will go, and who will stay."

After he had left my tent, I threw off my outer garments and stretched out on my narrow cot to think. The mere mention of his name had brought Lucius' sweet face into sharp focus. As I lay there brooding over what Sedonius had told me, that Lucius had joined the army and was somewhere in a hostile land, more than ever I felt the need to be with him, and to protect him from the horrors of war I knew only too well.

"Oh, Lucius," I murmured, gazing up through the gap in the tent roof, to the starry sky above me. "What madness have you become caught up in?"

If I were only free to go in search of him, I would. But my duty was here with my people. Their freedom was my goal, and I could not in good conscience sacrifice that ideal in order to satisfy my own personal longing. I could only pray to the gods that they might keep Lucius safe from harm—and that if in some future time or life we might meet again, there would be a chance of our finding happiness together.

You see, even princes and warriors can dream of the impossible.

✳ ✳ ✳ ✳ ✳

FLAVIUS

"Deny it though you will," I muttered to myself as I left his tent, "I know what is in your heart, Prince Callistus."

The proud Gaul would not admit to his fondness for Lucius, but I could see it in his eyes when I first mentioned his name. Now I knew I was right in my guess that Lucius had joined up simply to find a way to reunite with his lover. A crazy scheme, without a doubt, yet I felt a deep admiration for young Lucius, along with a certain envy. To love anyone that much must be a wondrous thing—a dangerous thing too, perhaps, but their time together must have been memorable at the very least for Lucius to undertake such a venture and sacrifice.

The Gaul was handsome, without a doubt, with a majestic bearing that spoke of his ability to lead, and be faithfully followed. How else could he command such fealty from his men? It was obvious they loved him, much as those ancient warriors had loved Alexander, despite his obsession with wishing to conquer all that lay before him.

Meanwhile, my fate, and that of my men, hung in the balance. *What would he decide?* I wondered. Instinctively I knew he would bid me stay, but what of the other officers? Their arrogance had angered him, and rightly so. They were fools to call him "barbarian" to his face. In Roman eyes, he was uncivilized, but here he was a prince, and beloved of his people. Those who mocked him might rue the day they meet him again, unless he was chained and at the mercy of the Roman Senate.

I had taken heed of his strength and superior leadership. I do not consider myself a coward, yet I would not care to meet Callistus face-to-face in battle. The man had been a gladiator, a hero in the arena, and he had survived the long, drawn out servile war under the leadership of Spartacus, the rebel slave. Better I be his friend than his foe. And better he never know of my sexual association with Lucius. Deny his affection he may, but it was there nevertheless, and if his jealousy was as fiery as his ardor, my life would be worth nothing.

× × × × ×

CALLISTUS

At daybreak, the guards brought the Roman prisoners before me to hear my decision. A night of confinement and rough sleeping conditions had done nothing to still the officers' arrogance. They stared defiantly at me as I stepped from my tent to address them. Only the Tribune, Flavius Sedonius, regarded me with any deference, while the soldiers themselves muttered among themselves with a nervous fear I could almost smell. I sought to make this as quick as possible. Now that the border had been contained, I was anxious to return to our stronghold, a two-day march from the border.

I signaled that Sedonius should approach me. "Tell the other officers they are free to go. If you wish to remain with your men, choose twenty of them. The rest can go. They will all leave their armor behind, however, and they must walk."

Sedonius winced at my words, but did not argue. However, as I expected, when he passed on my decision to the other officers, their voices were raised in anger.

"Perhaps you would rather face my archers' arrows than the rigors of a foot march," I yelled at them as they argued with Sedonius. They stopped shouting and waving their arms about in rage as I strode toward them, unsheathing my sword. "Go now," I said to the one who had called me "barbarian" earlier. "Go before you feel the point of this barbarian's sword. And tell your Senators that for every man held here, I demand ten thousand secertes in payment for their release." Then I added, for my own pleasure, "And twenty thousand for Tribune Sedonius!"

He smiled. "Only twenty thousand? You hold me cheaply, Prince."

"When you have chosen the men who must stay, hand them over to my guards, then join me in my tent." I walked away from the scowling officers, hoping that one day I would meet them again on the field of battle. Then we would see how much protection their hubris would afford them.

Sedonius was swift to join me, and I had some bread, cheese and wine brought to break our fasts. "Eat," I told him, and offered him a cup of wine that, though no doubt rough to Roman palettes, he drank with seeming appreciation. "Tomorrow we will leave for my home in the mountains. You and your men will accompany us, and be held there in our stronghold until the ransom is delivered—if indeed it ever is."

He nodded. "You know of course that the Senate will want to avenge this defeat. More legions will be sent to take back the border, and punish you."

I chuckled. "They have been trying to punish me for over three years, Sedonius. Ever since it was discovered I was one of the captains who led the army under Spartacus, it has been the Senate's wish that I be brought back to Rome in chains. So far, I remain at liberty—and I intend to do so for many more years."

He stared at me, the light of lust gleaming in his eyes. He leaned forward and put his hand on my bare thigh. I rose quickly, knocking his hand away.

"You are imprudent, Tribune. What makes you think I would, for one second, entertain a dalliance with you, or any man?"

"My apologies," he muttered, also standing. "You must know you inspire lust in others. I was too impetuous, Prince. Forgive me."

"You think that Lucius, the man you spoke of yesterday, and I were lovers, do you not?"

"Were you?"

"That is not your concern."

"True, but for Lucius' sake, I would wish it so. I could sense in his admiration for you that it seemed to extend beyond the merely platonic."

I sighed and sat down again, signaling that he should do so also. "Sedonius, I was a gladiator in the Capua arena. He was an admirer of mine, I will grant you that, but occasions for social intercourse were, of course, non-existent."

He seemed satisfied with my reply, for he nodded "Are you married, Prince Callistus?"

"My wife died a year ago."

"My condolences. Children?"

"None, nor do I have any parents. My father was killed in battle against your legions."

"But you are not the king?"

"My uncle holds that title. He and my father ruled jointly. I would not usurp his title for need of power. He legislates, I lead the army. It works well for us both. Before long, I must take another wife, and father a son. The people expect an heir..."

"Your uncle has no children?"

"He had a son. My cousin died in the same battle as my father. My uncle is an old man, the eldest of his brothers—and the only survivor." I grimaced ruefully. "You seem very interested in my life, Tribune. Are you a spy?"

He laughed lightly. "If I am, I'm not a very good one, imprisoned as I am at this moment, and for the foreseeable future. No, I find you interesting. Not at all the barbarian we Romans like to consider our enemies. I would like to think we might be friends."

"Friends? What kind of friend holds the other for ransom, with the possibility that he might die if it is not paid?"

He gazed into my eyes for a long moment before replying. "I do not think you will order my execution, Prince. Something about you tells me you are above such petty behavior. But if the ransom is not paid, and you find yourself forced to have me killed, I assure you I will hold no grudge against you. This is war, and we are enemies. My only regret would be that you have not been completely honest with me."

"What do you mean?"

"I mean, about you denying your affiliation with Lucius. He loves you, you know. Enough to give up an easy life of tutoring, and the comfort of his home and friends, to search for you. You may deny it, but I could see in your eyes the terror you felt for him when I told you he was on a campaign in Iberia."

"I will not speak of this with you," I said, my tone cold and dismissive. "Whatever fate befalls him, I cannot change. Our lives are too disparate, worlds apart. Even if..." I broke off, and waved him away impatiently. "Leave me now, Sedonius. Prepare your men for their march on the morrow. We will speak of this no more."

"Very well, Prince Callistus. Forgive me if I have offended you. That was not my purpose."

I watched him grimly as he saluted before leaving my tent. No doubt he had not meant to offend me, and in truth, I was not offended—only troubled once again at the thought of Lucius facing the rigors of army life. Not that I thought he couldn't handle it. Lucius was, if anything, stubborn and resilient. But if what Flavius Sedonius had said was true, that Lucius had enlisted only for the purpose of finding me, then even he might, by this time, be ruing the day he acted on such a foolhardy scheme. Even if he had accompanied Sedonius on his campaign to take the border of Cisalpine Gaul from us, he might have been killed in that first barrage of arrows we had sent on the Romans' heads. I shuddered at the thought of his body being skewered by an arrow shot by one of my own bowmen, or run through by a spear or sword.

"Why, Lucius?" I asked aloud. "Why did you do this foolish thing?" But I had asked him that same question when he faced the hardships of traveling to the camp of the servile army led by Spartacus. He had done it to see me then; only this time, his plans had come to naught, and only the gods knew now how he fared in enemy territory.

CHAPTER VI

LUCIUS

The home of Canto and his wife Selena was not an unpleasant prison. I dare say I was luckier than most of the other prisoners taken after our battle with the rebels. I worked hard in the house and in the garden, and my rewards were good meals and a comfortable bed. Canto himself was an affable jailer, allowing me to wander freely about the house and countryside. Of course, he knew I would be quickly lost if I tried to escape, and the chances of finding my way back to a Roman camp were practically negligible. To begin with, I had not a clue even in which direction to head. Add to that the fact that winter was fast approaching; already the wind had turned bitter and the evenings brought snow flurries. The thought of being stranded in some cave or under a tree while snow and hail covered me was not something I could look forward to.

From time to time, I would wonder how the other soldiers in my regiment were faring. Canto seemed to not have much news of them, saying only that they too had been sold into slavery, and were scattered around homes and farms in the town and countryside.

Perhaps in the spring, the Roman army would attempt another confrontation with the rebels, and this time led by a more able General than Mateus. Until then, I would have to bide my time, and make the best of my circumstances.

Canto's little daughters, Destina and Fortuna, were delights, and had taken a shine to me, following me about as I did my chores, and being quite attentive as I tutored them in Latin. The other rebels, friends of Canto's who visited him and his wife, regarded me with some curiosity—a Roman soldier who was also a teacher, and trusted enough by his owner to be left alone with the children. Quite often, I could hear Canto's neighbors question his wisdom in letting me have so much freedom. Of course, I could not understand all that was being said. I had only picked up a few words and phrases of the Iberian language, but the tone and body language of my critics was sufficient to tell me that they thought he would be better served were I tethered like an animal.

I found myself thanking the gods that they had given me to a man like Canto, rather than these ruffians he called friends.

The days, weeks and months passed slowly, but when spring arrived I began to look for some kind of rescue. Not that I wished Canto and his family any harm. If the Romans came to his house, I would defend him by telling the soldiers that I had been treated well, and that there was no need for retribution— at least, in Canto's home.

Of course, not a day had gone by when I did not think of Callistus, and the irony of my present position. I also wondered how Flavius had fared on his campaign against the Gauls. My heart would tremble at the thought of the two men meeting in pitched battle. It seemed to me that Flavius wouldn't have much of a chance against a warrior like Callistus, whom I knew could fight like a lion. I had seen him in action in the arena, and could only imagine his skill and the strength of his determination when defending his homeland.

At night when I lay on my narrow bed with its mattress of straw, my mind would take fanciful flight, and I would be with him once more, locked inside the power of his embrace, his lips caressing my skin, his manhood filling me to completion. I knew I moaned his name out loud on many occasions when my need for him became so great that I would grasp my own hard flesh, and bring myself release, all the while bringing his beautiful face and body into such sharp focus I could almost believe he was there with me. Not by one tiny particle had the image of his perfection faded from my mind, despite the long years that had passed since last I saw him. If I lived to be an old man, and never saw him again, he would haunt my memory forever as the young and vibrant warrior I had once known, and loved with all my heart.

But spring brought no sign, nor even word of an approaching Roman army. Perhaps the Senate had deemed it too costly, in both men and money, to punish the rebels for their defeat of Mateus' legions. That seemed to be the general consensus of opinion bandied about by those that visited Canto's home. There was a sense of accomplishment among the populace. Of having plucked the Roman eagle's wings, and still living to tell the tale. I could have mentioned that it was unlike Rome to allow its nose to be rubbed in the dirt and not seek vengeance, but why bother. My words would hardly have been deemed of any value.

And then it happened, and when it did, it was awful—and over so fast that those who survived would swear the enemy had descended from the skies, and not marched hundreds of miles through open countryside to reach them. The truth is, the Roman generals used subterfuge to deceive the rebels, dressing the advance guard in merchant's clothing, hiding their armor and weapons in the wagons that those who saw them approach thought carried goods to trade and purchase. The ruse worked with cold efficiency. Those closest to the wagons being unloaded of their supposed goods were cut down in a matter of minutes, the "goods" turning out to be swords, spears and axes that laid waste to the crowds of men, women and children gathered in the town market.

I heard the screams of terror and rage from where I stood, frozen to the spot, in Canto's garden. I knew at once something terrible was happening. Canto and Selena, his wife, came rushing from the house, he carrying a sword, ready to defend his home.

"Lucius," he cried. "See to the children." Even then, though he must have known the Romans were attacking his people, he trusted me with the lives of his daughters. I sprinted toward the house, just as the frightened faces of the little ones appeared in the doorway.

"Inside," I yelled, bundling them indoors and slamming the door. My mind was in chaos. How could I join Canto in the defense of his home against my fellow countrymen? Yet, how could I let him, his wife and daughters, whom I had come to feel affection for, be slaughtered? The answers to my jumbled thoughts became meaningless as soldiers poured through the streets, killing everyone in sight. Three of them burst through the gates to Canto's house, killing him and Selena before he could even raise his sword. The mad gleam of bloodlust was in their eyes as they approached me. Sweet Juno, I thought, I am only one more rebel for them to kill.

"Wait," I yelled, holding out my arms to show I was not armed. "I am a Roman soldier kept hostage here after the last battle!" At first I thought they had not heard me, or could have given a fig for my outburst, for their stride did not slacken, nor did they lower their swords.

"Who else lives here?" one of them barked at me.

"Just two little girls. They cannot harm anyone..." I was pushed out of the way, the door flung open, and I stood, shuddering with horror as I heard the terrified screams of the little girls suddenly cut off in the moment of their deaths.

"They were just little girls," I whispered as the men left the house.

The soldiers glared at me from blood spattered faces. "Our orders are that no one lives," one said. "You can thank the gods you don't look like the rest of them."

"There are other Roman prisoners here," I said.

"They'll be all right if they identify themselves quick enough. You better come with us."

I followed them from Canto's garden, trying not to look at the dead, upturned face of my recent master. The rescue I had hoped for had come, but at a cost I had not imagined. In my foolishness, I had supposed I could save them from the sword, but once again death had come too swiftly for it to be avoided.

The streets we passed through were littered with the bloody bodies of the fallen, but it was the market place that had been turned into a scene of horror. Everywhere I looked, bodies upon bodies, cut to pieces; the stench of blood and spilled entrails pervading the air, making me want to retch and puke my morning meal upon the ground. I listened to the soldiers' talk of the rebel army streaming from the surrounding hillsides to aid the townsfolk, and being annihilated by the Roman legions that had marched through the night behind the vanguard of soldiers disguised as merchants. Victory and vengeance were complete, with no prisoners taken. All had been put to the sword.

I, and a handful of other soldiers taken prisoner by the rebels, were marched in front of the officers and berated for our dismal performance of some months before. It was their considered opinion that because of our ineptitude, hundreds of Roman lives had been needlessly lost, a vast amount of money had been spent by the Senate to rectify our misdeeds, and we should consider ourselves lucky that we were not to be executed on the spot.

I listened to this litany of nonsense with my head bowed, like the others, as if in shame. When the ranting had ceased, I raised my head. "May I speak?" I asked.

"No, you may not!" an officer barked at me.

"Wait," An amused voice came from behind him. "Let him have his say."

I tried to see who had spoken, but the angry officer's big body blocked my view, so I braced myself for the inevitable punishment that would follow my words.

"You are all here today," I began, trying to keep the anger out of my voice, "not because of our inability to defend ourselves in battle, nor because of our *ineptitude*, as it was stated earlier. The rebels defeated us because of the incompetence and hubris of the man who led us—General Mateus. If he had been more the soldier, more aware of his enemy's cunning and bravery, and less enthralled by his own vanity, we might have won the day. Instead, he was preoccupied with having me write down his every vapid and boring opinion of army strategies, none of which, I may add, was ever agreed upon by any of his officers."

There was prolonged silence after my little speech, then the officer who had harangued us before stepped forward, his face red with rage. "How dare you, private? You will be flogged for this—"

"Wait." The same amused voice, but now tinged with some impatience, interrupted the officer's tirade. "Step over here, soldier."

Gritting my teeth, I did as I was bid, and saluted the officer who rose from his seat outside his tent, towering over me by at least a full head.

"What is your name, private?"

"Lucius Tullius, sir," I replied, looking into his eyes. Piercing blue eyes. He looked somewhat familiar.

"I am General Sedonius."

"Se... Sedonius, sir? I stammered. "I know a Tribune Sedonius... Flavius..."

"My son." He looked at me keenly. "Ah, yes. Lucius Tullius. He spoke of you..." He beckoned an officer over. "Dismiss the men. I will talk to this man in private." He indicated that I should follow him into his tent, where he bade me sit.

"I believe it was my son who recommended you for the position of Mateus' secretary," he said, settling himself behind a large table strewn with maps.

"It was, sir. Flavius... I mean, Tribune Sedonius was very helpful in securing that position for me."

He smiled thinly. "You still think that, after what has happened to you?"

"Well, I don't blame him for my capture, sir. He could not have foreseen that."

"Nor his own, I daresay."

"I beg your pardon?"

"Flavius is a prisoner of the Gauls. They are holding him, and several others, for ransom. Word of his capture was brought to me just before I set out on this campaign."

"I am sorry to hear that, General. You must be very worried."

"Yes. It is my intention that, when I return to Rome, I will mount a search and rescue campaign to find him, and bring him home."

"You will not pay the ransom?"

His eyes narrowed as he stared at me. "He is being held by barbarians, Lucius. They cannot be trusted to turn him over even if I paid the ransom. No, I intend to save my son, and his men—and destroy this upstart Prince Callistus, who holds him prisoner."

I stared at him, stunned, my mouth dry with shock. "*Prince* Callistus?"

He barked out a laugh. "Yes, you may sound surprised. These barbarians fancy themselves as princes and kings, when they are no more than savages and wild beasts, strutting around in the stolen finery of their pillaging and thievery."

He went on talking, but I was no longer listening. Flavius was a prisoner, being held by Callistus, *Prince* Callistus. Callistus was a prince. Of course, I had known all along that he was a man of substance and worth. I had known it from the very beginning. I had thought him majestic, and I had been correct.

"...So you see, that is all they understand..." The General's words invaded my seething mind. "They can be given no quarter. Just like the Iberian rebels, I will see every last one of them put to the sword."

"Sir?" I interrupted. "I would like to volunteer for your campaign to rescue Flavius."

"Good lad!" Sedonius beamed at me. "You shall be my secretary, but I promise, I will not ask you to fill page upon page of my vapid opinions." He laughed, well pleased with his joke, and as I joined in the laughter my mind raced ahead to the day when I would cross the border into Gaul, and finally come face to face with the man I loved more than life itself—Prince Callistus.

CHAPTER VII

66 B.C.

LUCIUS

Upon my return to Rome, I found that there was to be a two-week period before the campaign to rescue Flavius and his men, so I requested leave to return home in order to visit my mother and sisters. I found my mother well and happy, content with her new husband and home. My sister Lucia, and her handsome husband Cassius, greeted me warmly. They had the air of those few who are fortunate enough to find love in an arranged marriage, their happiness now made complete by the fact that Lucia was with child.

Unfortunately, my little sister Julia was, in my opinion, being spoiled to the point of foolishness. Perhaps the rigors of military life, being held prisoner and seeing little children slaughtered, had made me more cynical, but I disliked what Julia was fast becoming—a smart-mouthed and manipulative vixen who, when grown to marriageable age, might prove to be a shrew of a wife. I could only hope that as she grew up she would learn to value the good fortune of being Gaius' adopted daughter.

I had kept Rufus on as caretaker of my house, and he proved to be what I had always considered him—a reliable servant and good friend, keeping the house and garden in pristine condition, and welcoming me home with a belly-filling meal of stewed beef and onions and a pitcher of wine. I asked him to join me at the table, and he spent the evening listening to my war stories, and getting quite drunk along with me.

Petronius, of course, came to me every day, spending hours with me, and often the night. His affection for me, and mine for him, was unsullied by my absence. He had either forgotten or forgiven our last conversation before I left to join the army. Indeed, it seemed that his ardor had grown stronger, and I was hard pressed to keep him satisfied. For reasons that even I could not quite fathom, I was always able to distinctly separate my feelings for Petronius and Callistus. Never did I feel ashamed of the sex I shared with Petronius, despite the fact that my heart belonged to another man. His need for solace and affection was something that I could give him unconditionally, but what I gave of myself to him was very different from that given and received between Callistus and I.

That first night he was full of questions about how I felt when I discovered I was not joining the campaign to Gaul, and was I afraid when the rebels attacked the legion. I answered honestly.

"Yes, I was afraid," I told him. "But in the heat of battle, the instinct for self preservation takes over, and one finds strength, if not courage, to defend oneself. I was lucky though. I would be dead, had it not been for a fellow soldier's intervention." He wanted to hear all of that, and more, and something akin to awe was in his expression as he listened in rapt silence. When I had finished, he laid his head on my chest and held me in a warm embrace.

"I am so glad you're back safe and sound," he murmured. "When you left, I cursed myself for the bitter words I spoke to you."

I kissed his brow and stroked his dark hair. "You and I will always be friends, Petronius, no matter where our lives take us."

"And Callistus, will you go in search of him again?"

"I have volunteered for the next campaign to Gaul. Flavius is a prisoner there, and his father, General Sedonius, is leading an army to rescue him and his men being held for ransom."

"Why not just pay the ransom?" Petronius asked. "Why risk more lives when money would suffice?"

"It is matter of principle for the General, I think. He means to teach the Gauls a lesson."

"Even though they might kill his son when they see Sedonius leading an army?"

"Callistus holds Flavius prisoner. I would wager everything I have that he would not allow that to happen. He is a prince, Petronius."

"In *your* eyes, he is a god."

"No, I mean he really is a prince—Prince Callistus of the Helvetii."

"By the gods!" He lifted his head from my chest and stared up into my eyes. "When did you discover this?"

"The General told me in passing. I knew he was more than just a warrior, a man of worth. But a prince...?"

"Then is it not even more pointless now to seek him out? What can possibly come of your friendship? A prince, a ruler... he must be married, and may have children..."

I sighed as he babbled on. Of course, I knew all of what he said to be possibilities, but I would not rest until I knew it to be true. I told Petronius this, and although I could feel his irritation, he fell quiet. After a moment or two, he slipped his hand under my tunic and began to stroke my thighs and cover my neck with small kisses. We spoke no more of Callistus that night.

✳ ✳ ✳ ✳ ✳

Two weeks later, I was back in Rome, reporting to General Sedonius and taking up my duties as his secretary. It wasn't long before I came to the realization that Sedonius, although unlike General Mateus in that he was not intent on having me write down every word he uttered for posterity, had his own share of arrogance. It was rumored that the Senate had offered to pay the ransom for the release of Flavius and his men, but the General would not hear of it. It was his goal to punish the "barbarians" and teach Callistus a lesson. It shook me to hear the name of the man I loved uttered with such loathing by my superior officer—and the man with whom I spent so much of my time.

Very quickly, I came to hate General Sedonius.

Of course, I kept my hatred for the man hidden from him, affording him a quiet courtesy that he seemed to take as respect. During the long days of our march northward, he left me pretty much to my own devices, calling on me only if there were reports he felt he should make for the record. At night, he would often invite me to sup with him and the other officers, and I became privy to some interesting snippets of information that I stored away in my memory for future use.

For instance, I discovered that Gaul was a much larger country than I had ever thought it to be, bigger in area than Italia, and of course, much wilder and more dangerous. If I was ever foolish enough to desert and go in search of Callistus on my own, I reckoned my chances of survival registered at about zero. For better or worse, I had to remain within the confines of the legion. I could only pray that if the Gauls engaged us in battle—and there was a very good chance they would—I would be spared either the sight of Callistus being dragged away in chains, or myself being led before him, a wretched prisoner condemned to death by his word.

Many times, I wondered about the sanity of what I had undertaken. If ever I should actually meet him again face to face, just what would his reaction be? And then again I wondered if Flavius, should he ever have a chance to converse with Callistus, might mention my name to him. For what reason, I could not imagine, but if he did, would he admit to knowing of me? Or would he merely wave off any knowledge of my existence? All these thoughts came to plague me at night after I had extinguished the lamp by my cot and lay listening to the snores of my fellow soldiers. And then I was gripped by the fear that Flavius just might mention of our tryst in the woods. My blood would run cold at the thought of what Callistus might make of my infidelity—would he be filled with disgust, or after three years would he even care? I was unsure which emotion, or lack of one, would distress me more.

One bleak and chilly morning, I was called to the General's tent, and found already there all his officers gathered, their faces grim with the anticipation of what could only be the news of battle. The Gauls had sighted our advance party and had ambushed them, killing all the men, and sending their corpses back as a warning that we should advance no further. Naturally, Sedonius and his officers wanted confrontation with the enemy even more now, particularly as one of the dead centurions was the son of a high ranking officer of our legions. Preparations were made for an immediate advance into enemy territory in the hope that we would engage, and defeat, the Gallic force positioned there.

I began to feel the excitement that was invigorating the troops, even though my excitement stemmed from a different emotion. Soon, no matter what, I would find myself in the midst of battle, and maybe, just maybe, able to find my way into the camp, or stronghold, where Callistus dwelt.

"Lucius!" The sharp voice of General Sedonius brought me from my constant daydreams. "Attend me. I have some scribblings for you to undertake. Should I die in the conflict, I need my wife to know how to appropriate the gold I have stored up over the years."

It was his way of saying he was writing his will. Not something that filled me with optimism. His ardor for battle seemed to have diminished since the defeat of the advance guard, and even though his officers were adamant that the Gauls must be punished for this humiliation, I could sense in Sedonius a lack of purpose. Just as I had thought, he was all wind and no backbone. I could only hope that his son had more fortitude to withstand his captivity.

✹ ✹ ✹ ✹ ✹

FLAVIUS

Prince Callistus came to see me at daybreak. From the grim look on his face I knew that whatever news he was bringing me was not wrapped in good fortune.

"Your Romans are encamped on the other side of the border," he informed me, tersely. "Word has come to me that the advance body was wiped out to a man—no prisoners taken. I have also learned that the General leading the main force is none other than your namesake—a General Sedonius."

I gasped with shock. My father was leading an army here? Why had he not paid the ransom?

"You are surprised." Callistus sat, indicating that I do the same. "This man is kin to you?"

"My father," I said quietly, shaking my head. I looked at Callistus bleakly. "Why, when he could have paid the ransom without noticing it gone?"

"Perhaps he is not as rich as you thought him to be."

"He is richer than half the Senate!" I protested. "No, this is a matter of pride with him. To show you that Rome will not be intimidated, no matter whose sons you imprison."

"A man of character then," he said mildly.

"You would think so, given what he has undertaken, but I know my father."

"Meaning?"

"You said the advance guard has been cut down, no survivors. This will give him pause, he will reconsider his plan of action."

Callistus gazed at me without understanding. "You mean he will consult with his officers on how best to defeat us."

"No, Prince, he will withdraw. He might offer to pay the ransom, but he will not now engage you."

Now it was his turn to draw a breath of surprise. "But the other officers, his men having come all this way, and now not to fight?"

"I know it seems ridiculous to you, but unless his men can change his mind, he will not cross the border."

"Are you saying your father would face the dishonor of cowardice?"

I looked away from his steady gaze. *Was* that what I was saying? I had not, before this, thought of my father that way, but the defeat of the advance guard may have shown him that perhaps he was not as prepared to face the Gallic army as he had thought. A conversation I had once overheard came back to me at that moment. It seemed that once before, when faced with a similar situation, my father had hesitated and only the goading of his next-in-command had spurred him on. If, this time, his officers were not strong enough to encourage him to go forward, his hesitation would be seen as weakness among his troops—and the enemy, who no doubt stood poised and ready for battle.

"My father is not a coward, Prince Callistus," I said, in his defense.

"Well, we shall test his mettle. I plan on marching to join the army that guards the border. You, and your men, will accompany me. If your father offers to pay the ransom, I will honor the terms I originally set down. If not, we shall engage *him*, with no more delay."

I nodded my understanding, and in truth could find no fault with his plan. His enemies stood in vast array at the border to his land. He would be a weak leader indeed if he did not take action, and Callistus was far from weak. In the months of my imprisonment, I, and most of my men, had formed a deep respect for the man, and for the loyalty he invoked among his people. We had not been treated harshly—far from it. Our quarters, though Spartan-like, were clean and the food plentiful enough. Occasionally, Callistus had asked me to dine with him, and I had been careful not to drop any mention of Lucius into our conversation.

He looked at me now expectantly, as though he thought I might have some objection, but truthfully, I could find none. He was simply doing what any able commander would do, and with the confidence and assurance those who followed him fully expected. Not for the first time, I envied Lucius his time spent with this man, and wished that I could serve under his banner. Traitorous thoughts perhaps, but ones I could feel no shame in having.

✗　✗　✗　✗　✗

LUCIUS

General Sedonius dismissed me after I had finished the "scribblings," as he called my work. His officers surged into his tent as I was leaving, eager to hear of his decision, and to reverse it should it not align with their own. I knew they were not about to allow him to call off this campaign. They had come too far to return without freeing Flavius along with the other hostages, and battling the Gauls, punishing them for their insurrection.

I walked to the far side of our encampment where I could, as I had done day after day, look across the border and wonder if Callistus had arrived with his army. I knew he would come eventually, and just to be able to catch a glimpse of him I thought would be enough. Then I would feel that all this upheaval in my life had been worthwhile. I turned, startled, as a cry went up from within the camp.

"To arms... We march within the hour..."

So the officers had prevailed, and we were to meet the Gallic army in force. My heart pounded with excitement as I raced to my quarters to put on my armor and pick up my weapons. Everywhere, men ran about in preparation for the battle to come. Horses were rounded up and equipped with the cavalry riders' saddles and bridles. Officers roared commands, horses whinnied and stamped their hooves in expectant readiness while the clank of heavy armor and weapons pervaded the air.

Out of this chaos came order, and soon the troops were lined up for inspection, and the cavalry at the head of the legion ready for the command to head out. I took my place amid one of the cohorts, my gladius banging against my thigh as we started to march forward. So it was now, that for which I had come so far was now here, and I could not have been more excited, nor afraid, if I had tried. Not a fear of dying, that comes to us all, but the fear of seeing the man I loved facing me as the enemy, or worse still, dead on the field of battle. What horrors awaited me, I had no way of knowing then—which probably was as the gods planned it.

✶ ✶ ✶ ✶ ✶

CALLISTUS

The Romans, as always, provided a magnificent spectacle as they advanced across the border.

"Will you allow parley?" Flavius asked, at my side.

I glanced at him and shrugged. "They show no sign of wishing to talk," I replied. "The time for meeting would have been when they were on the other side of the border. However, I will order no attack yet."

"You mean to let them pass, then surround them, do you not?" he asked, shading his eyes from the bright morning sun.

"Yes. They seem to be unaware of our presence." As I spoke, I could almost hear Flavius grind his teeth in frustration. Of course, his every instinct would be to warn his fellow countrymen of the fact they were marching into a possible trap. I put my hand on the hilt of my sword in an unmistakable sign of warning to him.

He met my eyes with a steady gaze and said, "If I could but talk with my father, perhaps this day would see no bloodshed."

"Then go to him," I said, ignoring his gasp of surprise. "Tell him that if he turns his army around and leaves here in peace, I will not attack. You will return with his reply. I will hold your men here as surety."

Now I knew that in the mind of a Roman General, twenty men were of little sacrifice if he decided to ignore my offer and lead his men into battle. Still, Flavius deserved this chance, I thought. He had proven himself to be a man of honor, and I trusted that he would return, one way or another. I signaled to my men that Flavius was to be allowed safe passage as he cantered through their ranks and down the hillside toward the Roman army. Thalanius, my second-in-command, spurred his mount toward me.

"What's the plan?" he asked, frowning.

"I'm giving Flavius a chance to speak with the Roman general. Apparently his father leads the legions below us."

"You trust him to return?"

"We still hold twenty of his men." I smiled wryly. "I know there is a chance he might sacrifice them to save his own skin, but I don't see that in the man. He may fail in his mission, but I think he will return."

"And if he does not?"

"Then either he could not convince his father to pay the ransom, and is being held against his will, or he has betrayed us, and his men." I shrugged. "Either way, we will know soon enough. Tell the men to stand at the ready. The signs of an imminent attack by the Romans will be easy to discern from this vantage point."

✷   ✷   ✷   ✷   ✷

FLAVIUS

I hailed the cohort of soldiers as I approached them, identifying myself as a Roman tribune, and the son of General Sedonius. My father seemed surprised to see me, and did I also detect a look of relief in his eyes, that went beyond mere happiness in the fact that his son was still alive and well?

"Flavius!" he cried as he embraced me. "Thank the gods those devils have not harmed you."

"They will not attack if you pay the ransom for me and the men they still hold," I told him after he had bade me sit, and ordered wine to be brought to his tent.

"But can we trust them?"

"Prince Callistus I believe to be a man of his word."

My father looked at me sharply. "He is a savage, Flavius, a barbarian without ethics or honor."

"I don't believe that to be so," I replied calmly. "I have been his hostage now for close to six months, and he has treated me and my men fairly at all times. He could have had us tortured on a daily basis if he'd wished. And, dare I say it? If he were ever a prisoner of the Senate, I don't think he'd be treated with the same respect."

His face darkened. "Be that as it may, I don't think my officers will agree to simply turn around and go home. They have come prepared for battle and booty. Most of what these barbarians now own, they took from Romans."

"So, you're saying you will not pay the ransom?"

"We met last night to discuss this, and as I said, the officers are against it."

"Then I must return and tell him of your decision."

"Return?" He stared at me in amazement. "Are you mad?"

"That was a part of our agreement—that I would return to him with your answer. And besides, he still holds my men hostage!"

"Oh, that... if as you say he is a man of honor, he will execute them painlessly."

I stared at him, speechless with shame at his lack of consideration for his fellow Romans. "I cannot allow that, I'm afraid," I said through gritted teeth.

"You have no choice, Flavius," he snapped. "I forbid you to leave this camp, and if you refuse to obey my orders I will have you confined until you see sense!"

"Arrest me, then," I cried, rising and striding from his tent. I had almost reached my horse when I heard him yell, "Hold him!" and several guards grabbed me and hauled me back to where he stood, trembling with rage.

"You would dare disobey me?' he seethed. "Your father, *and* the commanding officer here? Have you forgotten what the penalty for disobedience is?"

"No Father, I have not forgotten. Flog me, then, if that is your will. But I will not turn my back on my men."

His eyes flicked away from mine, and I could tell he was ashamed of what he now felt compelled to do. But he could not also now lose face in front of the men.

"Confine him to quarters until further notice," he growled, then turned away from me and disappeared into his tent.

The guards led me away, but one of them asked me under his breath, "What's all that about then? What men are you talking about?"

"There are twenty Roman soldiers being held hostage by the Gauls," I replied. "I came down here to ask they be ransomed and set free. It seems that they are of little consequence to my father and his officers."

"Well, can you trust those savages to release them even after they got the ransom?"

"I think so..."

The guard fell silent, and no more was said while I was marched through the camp to a tent where I would be quartered, under guard, until my father decided what to do with me.

"Flavius!"

I jerked my head in the direction of the cry, and saw Lucius, in full armor, staring at me with shock and wonderment. He ran over to where I stood flanked on either side by the guards.

"I mean, Tribune Sedonius," he said panting slightly. "Why are you under arrest?"

"His *father* ordered it," one of the guards said. "And be off, there's no conferring with prisoners."

"But..." Lucius looked as if he were about to argue the point.

"I'll get word to you later, Lucius," I said quickly.

He nodded, and watched silently as I was led away.

✵   ✵   ✵   ✵   ✵

LUCIUS

"Why would the General have his own son arrested?" Marius, one of my fellow soldiers with whom I had just been on patrol, gave me a curious look. "Isn't he the reason we've come all this way?"

I nodded, but was unable to answer the question. Why indeed would he have Flavius arrested? "I don't know," I said. "But I'm sure I'll be asked to inscribe what has taken place at the officer's meeting that's bound to follow. I'd better go and report at the General's quarters." With that I left him, walking quickly toward Sedonius' tent, my mind working on all the possibilities that might have led to his son's arrest.

As I had guessed, Sedonius had called a meeting of his officers, and he waved me in when I appeared at the entrance to his tent.

"Lucius, we'll need notes taken," he said sharply. It was obvious he was in a foul mood, so I quickly pulled off my helmet, unbuckled my sword belt and breast plate, and gathered my writing things in readiness for the meeting.

I hesitated for a moment, then said, "Sir, I just saw Flavius being led away by the guards..."

He swung round, a dark look of warning on his face. "This matter will be resolved by myself and the other officers, Private Tullius," he barked at me. "You will merely transcribe what is said—and then forget it. D'you understand?"

"Of course, General." I sat down on my writing stool and averted my eyes from his. The man was belligerent at the best of times, and when in one of his moods, could be irrational. I wondered how his officers could stand it sometimes. They began to filter in one by one, looking grim and unsure of what Sedonius would require of them. Of course, they must have heard the rumors already. My mind went to thoughts of Callistus; he was never far from my mind, but now that I was about to hear his name spoken in anger and disgust, I wondered if I would be able to stand it.

"My son, Flavius, has returned unharmed from the Gaul's captivity." The General's announcement was greeted with polite congratulatory sounds from the officers gathered around him. "However, I have had to confine him to quarters in order to prevent him returning to his captors."

"But why would he want to do such a foolhardy thing?"

Sedonius fixed the officer who had asked with a beady eye. "Because he feels some misplaced loyalty to the men he left behind. Because we won't pay the ransom to have them released."

"Your son is an honorable man," an officer I recognized as Tribune Cassius Egnatius said quietly. "And for that he is now a captive of his own people."

"For his own good!" Sedonius spat, his face aflame.

"What is it you plan to do, General?"

"Engage and destroy the Gauls, once and for all—along with that devil, *Prince* Callistus of the Helvetii."

My hand trembled at the mention of his name, and I dropped my stylus. As I bent to retrieve it, a guard entered the tent, saluting sharply.

"What is it?" Sedonius rasped.

"One of the hostages has been returned. He says he has a message for you, General." As one, the officers jumped to their feet, all looking to Sedonius for his orders.

"Then bring him here, at once." Sedonius looked slightly nervous as he waited for the man to be ushered in. He was young, younger than I, and looked to be well fed. He was wearing a homespun tunic, and his hair had grown long during his captivity.

"*Salve*, General…" His salute was still military sharp.

Sedonius asked in his usual clipped manner, "You have a message from the Gauls?"

"Yes, General. Prince Callistus is willing to let your army return over the border without interference, if you leave all the gold you carry as ransom for your son and the rest of us. He says he knows you have arrested Tribune Flavius, and does not pretend to understand why, as the Tribune is your son. But he is willing to overlook this apparent lack of familial affection and consider it a Roman problem."

One of the officers gasped, another sniggered then coughed, while Sedonius glared at the soldier with cold eyes. "There is no reply, of course," he said. "You may join the men in their quarters. Dismissed."

"But sir, the other men's lives depend on your answer!"

"I said there is no reply!" Sedonius leaped to his feet, his face scarlet with rage. "Dismissed! Join the regiment, or be put to death for desertion!"

A low murmur of discord came from the officers as the soldier stumbled from the tent. Tribune Egnatius fixed the General with a look of disdain. "Hardly the way to treat a loyal soldier, General, and one who feels for his fellow hostages. Such a thing will not sit well with the men when word of it goes around the camp, as it surely will."

"You question my authority?" Sedonius was fairly purple with rage by this juncture.

"I question your judgment, General, as I am sure all here do. It is obvious that the Gaul's leader is giving you a choice—pay the ransom or fight. Either will suffice as far as I am concerned, but arresting your son and threatening a messenger with death is not the way to go about it. Send word to the Gaul, one way or the other, but do it in a rational manner!"

For a moment I thought Sedonius was going to order Egnatius arrested, but seeing the grim looks on the other officers' faces may have caused him to stay that rash impulse. He let out a long breath through pursed lips, then nodded.

"So be it," he said, his voice cold and imperious. "Have a messenger sent to reply to the Gaul's demands. The answer will be, no ransom, and if they execute any Roman soldiers, they will pay the price a hundred-fold."

"Sir..." I stood up and addressed Sedonius with what I hoped was a firm and clear voice. "I would volunteer to take that message to the Gauls, and offer myself as hostage for the release of the other men."

Sedonius gazed at me as if he had forgotten I was in his presence. "You?" He let out a short laugh. "You consider yourself of equal value to nineteen seasoned soldiers?"

"No, I do not," I replied calmly. "I am merely requesting that I be allowed to take your message to the Gaul... to Prince Callistus. It so happens that I am acquainted with the man."

"What?"

There was a stir of interest from the officers in the room, while Sedonius stared at me with disbelief.

"He was a gladiator in the arena at Capua, my hometown. I saw him fight many times, and I was enlisted by Lentullus Batiatus, the *lanista,* to mediate for him when the gladiators rioted due to one of them being victimized and beaten by the guards. I spoke with Prince Callistus—but at that time I did not know him to be of royal blood..."

"Royal blood!" Sedonius laughed his contempt. "He is a barbarian without a drop of royal blood in his veins."

"Be that as it may," Egnatius interrupted. "This young man may have an edge." He looked at me with shrewd eyes. "You think he will remember you?"

"I think so. Before the gladiators rebelled under Spartacus, I was asked again to mediate, and was there when they took over the *ludo,* and threw Lentullus and his guards out. He gave me safe passage. Yes, I think he will remember me."

Egnatius turned his eyes to Sedonius and shrugged. "What do we have to lose? Send him, I say. Perhaps the Gaul will listen to reason, and release our men." He looked back at me. "You do realize that you stand to lose your life."

"I remember Prince Callistus to be a fair man," I replied. "I think I can persuade him to at least release the hostages."

"Something that my son could not," Sedonius sneered. "Yet you think because you spoke to the barbarian some years ago, he will listen to you." He snorted his derision. "Very well, go and *mediate.* In the meantime I will enlist the aid of another secretary!"

Egnatius rolled his eyes and beckoned me forward. He put his hand on my shoulder and led me from the tent. "You're a brave lad," he said. "A pity that our General has not the grace to acknowledge it. We will send you out tomorrow at dawn. The gods be with you."

Of course, that night I could not sleep for the excitement of knowing that I would at last see Callistus again. I could only hope that Flavius, should he discover my intentions, would not make an issue of this, request an audience with his father, and demand that *he*, Flavius, be sent as the messenger. What would he make of my volunteering? Had he guessed of my true feelings for Callistus in the short time we had talked of him?

But soon, none of that would matter. As dangerous as I knew my offer to meet with Callistus would be, I felt secure in the knowledge that he would not harm me. As I lay there in my narrow bed, my heart pounded as I envisioned his expression of surprise, and I hoped delight, on seeing me again. My mind took flights of fancy, imagining the feel of his arms about me, his lips on mine, his sweet breath filling my mouth, devouring my senses…

✖ ✖ ✖ ✖ ✖

CALLISTUS

I knew the Romans would take some time to deliberate on my offer—I also knew what the answer would be. The Roman hostages had looked at me nervously when I told them of my plan to send one of them with my message. They knew the time of reckoning was near, and like good soldiers were prepared for whatever might befall them, but with the hope that they might live to fight another day, and even return home when the battle was over.

It was a surprise to me when one of my men ran to my tent and breathlessly informed that a Roman emissary was making his way toward our encampment. My men were restless, eager for battle, and tired of my efforts to bring them the ransom they had thought was theirs when we held Flavius hostage. They wanted a speedy resolution to this standoff—and frankly, so did I.

"Bring me my horse," I told the man. "I will meet this emissary, and be done with him quickly." After all, the answer would be either gold or battle. How long could it take to hear those words?

Belenus was brought to me, saddled and bridled, and as I swung myself up onto his back, I thought for the thousandth time of Lucius, and how he had looked astride the steed on the day I sent him back to his family. I hoped he had forgiven me for taking Belenus from him after our last night together. I urged Belenus forward, and the men gathered behind me to watch what they imagined would be a very short conference with the emissary that now cantered toward the camp.

I knew him before he got near, and for a moment my heart stopped in my chest and my breath caught in my throat.

"*Lucius...*"

His name was torn from my lips as my eyes took in every part of his face and form. Despite the fact that he was wearing a Roman soldier's uniform, I could tell he had not changed one whit in the years that had passed since our last all-too-brief meeting. As he drew abreast of me, I could see those same shining brown eyes now fixed upon mine, and the same sweet smile I remembered each time he looked at me.

Oh, Lucius, what have you done? Why are you here on this field that will soon be covered in blood, and the bodies of men? But of course, I knew the reasons, and as he gazed at me with an expression of longing and love, I felt my loins burn with lust, and the need to crush him in my arms and cover his face and body with my lips.

"Hail, Prince Callistus..." His melodious voice rang out, I knew, for the benefit of my men who stood behind us watching our every movement. "I am Lucius Tullius, secretary to General Sedonius, and bear you a message from him, for your ears only."

I nodded, and turned my horse around, signaling that he should follow. We rode, side by side, through the press of fighting men, who regarded him with deep suspicion, and not a little hostility. If I was going to save him, I would have to tread very carefully. I pulled Belenus up to a halt outside my tent, dismounted and bade him do the same. I turned to face the curious expressions of my men.

"This man has brought me a message only I can hear," I told them. "When I am satisfied that it bears merit, I will share it with all of you. Till then, man your positions, and watch for Roman treachery."

The men dispersed, our horses were led away, and I took his arm, leading him into the privacy of my quarters. For a moment, we stood gazing at one another, and then he removed his helmet. I stared at his shorn head. Gone was the tumble of boyish curls I remembered holding between my fingers and brushing from his forehead. Instead, his short military haircut clearly defined the fine chiseled cut of his features, sharpened now by maturity. My Lucius was no longer a boy, but a man in his prime—a beautiful man, and one for whom my lonely yearning was now transformed into a deep-seated, carnal desire.

"I feel that I should kneel in your presence," he said softly, but with the hint of a smile.

"Did my title surprise you?" I asked.

"No, for in my eyes you were always a prince."

We fell into each other's arms, our mouths meeting in a kiss that sent my senses spinning out of control. Armor, tunics, leggings and undergarments were stripped away as we fell upon one another like hungry animals. For indeed we were, hungry for the feel and taste of each other's lips and bodies, so long missed, so often dreamed of.

"Lucius," I breathed, my mouth on his, my hands cupping his face, pressing myself to him as if I had found shelter in a storm. His arms wound around my neck, holding our lips locked together. I could feel and taste the saltiness of his tears on his cheeks as he clung to me.

"Callistus, oh Callistus… how I have dreamed of this moment, longed for it every day of my life. I love you… never has my love for you faltered for one moment."

I crushed him to me, my mind racing with both the need for him, and the need to keep him safe. His sweet body pressed to mine filled me with a carnal lust that overwhelmed me, and drove from my thoughts everything but my need and longing for him. Four years of pent up desire to hold him once again in my arms, to feel his hot moist kisses, and the heat of his hard cock against mine, swept away all reason. He was here, and that was all that mattered. I lifted him into my arms and he wound his legs around my waist, holding me a willing prisoner in his embrace. I carried him to my bed and laid him down, covering his body with mine, cradling him in my arms, and showering his face and naked body with kisses hot from their urgency and passion. He clung to me, his taut, sweet body writhing beneath me, filling me with a desperate need to take him, to possess him, and to never let him out of my sight again.

The long years we had been parted seemed to disappear from my memory, and it felt as if it had been only yesterday since we last held one another and kissed with such intensity. Our last lovemaking had been made bittersweet by the knowledge that I had to leave him, and even though our time together again might be brief, I cast away all those thoughts, and gave myself up to the moment, to the joy of having him back in my arms. There was not a part of him I left unkissed, and when I took his hard, throbbing flesh into my mouth, the long sigh of ecstasy that escaped his lips was as the sweetest music to my ears.

I grasped the base of his cock, and lapped at the head, licking and savoring the steady stream of his essence that spilled over my tongue. I fondled his balls, and after moistening my forefinger, probed his sweet puckered hole, bringing moans of sheer pleasure from his throat. He bore down on my finger, drawing it deeper inside him, while his cock jumped in my mouth from the sensation.

His fingers tangled in my hair as he whispered, "Oh, Callistus, fuck me, please. Let me feel all of your cock inside me. I have lived only for this moment, when you will take me and make me yours again."

His plea set my loins on fire, but before I fulfilled his wish, I burrowed my face between his buttocks, spreading his cheeks, pushing at his hole with my tongue, using my saliva to ease my way inside him. His musky scent set my senses reeling. He writhed and squirmed under my tongue's strokes, grasping my hair even tighter and moaning aloud. I knelt between his legs and he brought them up and around my waist. His eyes were locked on mine, his smile proof of his love, and his willingness that I take dominion over him. I thrust forward, the head of my cock pushing past his resistance, desperate now to take him. His eyes widened with the shock of my invasion, but then his smile returned and his arms enveloped me, holding me close to him, his lips finding mine in an all consuming kiss. His hips thrust upward to meet me, and the intense rhythm we created filled us both with rapture. I plunged deeper, until my thighs pressed against his, and his moans of pleasure on my lips brought me an ecstasy beyond reason.

"Callistus..." His body arched under me, his legs tightened about me as he cried out my name. "Oh yes, my love!" He pushed upward hard against me, impaling himself on me down to the root.

"Lucius..." I gasped his name even as my body shuddered under the impact of my orgasm. I groaned aloud, and lifted him into my arms as I came, driving my cock even deeper inside him. He cried out and I felt his seed erupting from him, coating our fused torsos with its creamy heat. We remained like that, joined at the core, until the spasms of our mutual climax subsided. I lowered him onto his back and lay over him, licking at the still warm semen that covered his chest. His eyes, so full of love, met mine, and with a groan that was joy mingled with pain, I crushed him to me as if I would never let him go.

CHAPTER VIII

Lucius

As I lay in the warm shelter of his arms, I told the gods that if this was all I would ever receive from them in my life, then I was content. What I had prayed for, but thought impossible, had been gifted to me by their generosity, and even then, surrounded as we were by danger and animosity, I felt as if my destiny had been fulfilled. What had passed between us was everything I had ever dreamed of in the years we had been apart. And if it were possible, the reality had surpassed all my dreams.

His beauty was still there, despite the scar that marred his forehead, the scar I now traced with my fingertip, before stroking the rough light-colored stubble that covered his cheeks. My breath escaped from me in a long, shuddering sigh. The feel of his hard warm flesh under my hands caused my body to ache with desire, despite the tumultuous release I had experienced only minutes before. There would never be a time when I said "enough," for even if I lived another lifetime, I would never have enough of him.

He kissed my brow and my eyes, then whispered, "We must arise and give the men your news, such as it is." He stood and pulled me to my feet, holding me in his arms for a fleeting moment more before handing me my tunic. We dressed in silence. He helped me buckle my breastplate into place, and then, without a word, he strode outside to summon his second-in-command. While he was gone, I looked about me at the Spartan-like living quarters; at the bronze, studded shield that bore the marks of many battles, at the long sword that hung, sheathed, from its broad belt of leather and metal, and at the fur trimmed cloak that was flung over the back of a wooden chair.

So few princely belongings, I thought, but then only what I would have expected from a man like Callistus—worldly things would not impress him, only those which he needed to survive. Not for him the trappings or finery his position could have afforded him. I doubted whether a crown or diadem had ever adorned his head, or an ermine cloak swathed his body.

I looked to the tent flap as it parted and he entered, a tall, dark-haired and bearded man at his side. "Private Tullius, this is Thalanius, my second-in-command. I have told him you wish to offer yourself as hostage in place of the men we now hold captive. Unfortunately, he is of the opinion that such an exchange is of no value to us—and I have to agree with him."

Thalanius regarded me with suspicion. "What makes you think you are of equal value to the nineteen we now hold?"

I shrugged. "If by that you mean do I think myself equal to their value as fighting men, the answer is most assuredly I do not. However, my mother recently married a man of great wealth. I think I could persuade him to ransom me at a higher price than is asked for the soldiers you presently hold hostage."

Callistus' eyes widened for a moment at this piece of news. Of course, I had not had the time to tell him of my family's change of fortune.

Thalanius grunted, unimpressed. "Another wait for ransom that may never come." He turned to Callistus. "I say, send him back with a message for Sedonius. Pay up or prepare for battle. Why should we wait possibly for many weeks more on this pup's say so?"

I hid my smile and dared not meet Callistus' amused expression. Pup, indeed, and here I thought I looked the part of the stalwart soldier in my fine armor! I knew Callistus was about to agree with Thalanius. Despite his desire to keep me by his side, I could tell he was considering sending me back to the comparative safety of the Roman encampment.

"Better still," Thalanius added. "Send only his head back. That should be enough to tell the Romans we will not stand for any more stalling tactics. Fight or flee, is what I would tell them!" He gave me a grim smile. "Fear not, Roman, our prince does not believe in the barbaric methods of your leaders, more's the pity!"

Callistus clapped his hand on the man's shoulder. "I agree we should send him back, but with his head on his shoulders, and with one last message to the Roman General. We will give him twenty-four hours to deliver the ransom. If he refuses, the hostages will be executed, and we will attack his forces."

"Prince Callistus…" I bowed my head in deference to him. "Again, I would ask that you release the hostages and keep me here in their place. That way, you will receive the ransom you request—from my stepfather, if not from the General."

"We cannot wait that long, Private Tullius. Each day that the Roman army is on our land brings the people that much closer to danger. One way or another, this matter will be settled within twenty-four hours." He turned to Thalanius. "Tell the men to sharpen their swords and spears. I feel that at this time tomorrow they will be needing them."

Thalanius nodded and left the tent, without another glance my way.

Callistus and I gazed at one another in silence, then I said, "I wanted you to keep me close to your side."

"I know, and I would wish for it to be so, Lucius, but your offer has no value, except to me. The men see value in numbers—nineteen hostages instead of one."

"Then I would ask that you do not engage the Roman army," I pressed. "Offer a truce and the return of the hostages as a token of your word."

He shook his head. "There can be no truce between us and the Romans. They will not rest until they have conquered this land, and as long as I live, I will prevent that from happening. Lucius." He stepped forward and cupped my face in his big hands. His lips on mine were warm and gentle. "I will pray to the gods to keep you safe, and ask of them that we never meet on the field of battle."

I flung my arms about his neck and held his mouth on mine in a long and rapturous kiss. The heat between us was so intense that it took all of our self-control not to give in to the lust and desire that sprang from our loins, and our fast-beating hearts. He tore himself from me, and stepped back, panting slightly.

"You must go," he said hoarsely. "Go, before I throw all caution to the wind and beg you to stay with me forever."

"And that I would gladly do," I replied, tears welling in my eyes.

"I know. Oh, Lucius, I am at least grateful for the time we have had together. In my wildest imaginings I did not foresee it happen." His gaze dropped away. "Go now…"

I walked to the tent flap, then paused as I drew near him. "I love you, Callistus," I whispered. "In life or death, that will never change."

✺   ✺   ✺   ✺   ✺

FLAVIUS

I watched Lucius return to the camp and go directly to my father's quarters. My father had released me that morning, after I had given my word that I would not try to return to the Gaul's encampment. What would be the point, I thought, now that Lucius had gone to parley with Callistus? If he could not find a way to end this stalemate, no one could. I wondered how they had both felt on seeing one another again. Had they felt the spark of the long-lost love I was sure they shared those years ago? Had they managed to consummate that love before Lucius returned? I felt a quick rush of envy at the thought of them locked in each other's arms, their naked bodies joined together. The magnificent Callistus taking dominion over Lucius' lithe and virile body… I shook myself to dispel the vision that brought a discomforting heat to my face and body. Sighing, I made my way to my father's tent. The other officers were gathering there, summoned to hear what offer Lucius had brought, if any.

His eyes flicked my way, and he gave me a small smile as I entered and took my place with the other officers.

"So…" My father looked as impatient and frustrated as always. I had the feeling that this would be his last campaign. "The barbarian, did he have anything to say?"

Lucius nodded. "He has given us twenty-four hours in which to either deliver the ransom, for which he will set the hostages free, or to see our men executed. Our refusal of his terms will result in an immediate challenge to battle."

"What arrogance!" Father leaned back in his chair and glared around at us all.

"You think he will execute the men?" I asked

Lucius nodded again. "I think he must. Anything else his men would see as a sign of weakness on his part. I don't think he wants to have them killed, he is not blood-thirsty, but he may be forced to carry out the executions."

Tribune Egnatius asked, "Could you see the size of his army?"

"Formidable," Lucius replied. "In the tens of thousands, I would say."

"But undisciplined," my father snapped. "Ragged and naked savages who paint their bodies, and follow no man's orders."

"On the contrary…" Lucius now spoke more to us than to my father. "His men are well armed, and seem loyal to a man."

My father sneered, and laughed derisively. "How could you possibly tell that?"

"Because they have waited under his command for your answer for several days now, with seeming patience and good nature. Undisciplined men who follow no man's orders would be less inclined to be so patient."

My father's nostrils flared with anger. "You are insolent, Private," he rasped.

"But observant," Egnatius said, coolly. "So, do we pay, or fight?"

"There is no question of paying!" my father rasped. "I will not deal with this so-called prince anymore. Tomorrow morning we will prepare for battle, and show him what it is to feel the might of Rome's armies."

"Shall I convey that message to Prince Callistus?" Lucius asked, and to my mind with a shade too much hope.

"No, you shall not," my father barked. "There is no need to convey any message. They will see us advance and know what we intend."

"And the hostages?" I asked.

"If they die, it will be for the glory of Rome," he said, not looking at me. "Dismissed!"

"A small consolation," I murmured, turning away. Lucius and I left the tent together, walking rather aimlessly through the camp.

"Did he know you?" I asked, after we had walked in silence for some time.

"Yes, he knew me."

"Did you renew your pledge to one another?"

He looked at me and sighed. "I suppose the time for avoidance of the truth is past. Yes," his eyes held tears as he gazed at me, "it was as though we had never been parted. Flavius... I just don't know how I will get through the next day or so knowing that he and I are on opposite sides, and though I pray to the gods to prevent it, may meet on the battlefield. I know I sound like a traitor, but I could never raise my sword against him."

"Nor he against you, Lucius," I murmured.

"Can we defeat the Gauls?" he asked.

"In a pitched battle, yes. Our numbers far exceed his. But he is a cunning fighter, with many surprises we cannot always see coming. He will be prepared to deal with our superior forces. I would say the odds are evenly stacked."

He did not comment, so I asked, "Will he execute the prisoners?"

"If it were only up to him," he replied, "they would be safe, or at least returned to us. But I fear his men may insist they die, perhaps as a sacrifice before the battle."

"They will die bravely, but that is not the way for good men to die, without a sword in their hands." We had reached the perimeter of the camp, and we stood together, looking out into the darkness, at the lights from the fires of the Gaul's encampment.

"Are you wondering what he is doing?" I asked softly.

"As I have done each and every day since I first met him," he replied. "He has never left my thoughts, nor will he, no matter what the morrow brings. Their deaths, or ours, his or mine... If the gods take me, I will speak of him in their presence." He looked at me with those shining eyes of his. "I must apologize to you, Flavius."

"For what?"

"For using you as I did."

I smiled and touched his cheek gently with my fingertips. "If I was used, it was a sweet and memorable using, nonetheless."

He returned my smile. "It was not unpleasant."

I chuckled ruefully. "Faint praise, Lucius, but after spending time with your hero, I feel it would be foolish to compete with his prowess."

He fell silent, looking away from me, up into the hills where he knew his lover waited. Sadly, not for his return, but for the battle he knew Callistus must win at all costs, or lose everything he held dear.

CALLISTUS

Castes came to my tent with the news just after dawn. "The Romans are mustering for battle, Prince Callistus," he said, with some excitement. "Their camp is alive with preparations."

I rose and threw my cloak about me. "Send Thalanius to me."

"Yes, Prince," he ran to do my bidding, and as I dressed I knew that what I was about to do would anger Thalanius and many of the men.

Thalanius was at my tent in minutes, fully armored, his sword hung low from his hip as he favored it. The light of battle was in his eyes, but his smile faded as he listened to my order.

"Free the hostages... but why?" he demanded. "The men will not like this leniency."

"We were holding them for ransom," I said. "There is none. They are brave men, Thalanius, even if they are Romans. They do not deserve to die like dogs. This day will probably see them die anyway, but at least they will have a fighting chance."

He looked me in the eye for a very long time, and I began to wonder if he was about to defy me, but then he shrugged. "You are our leader, and right or wrong, I will do as you bid. Perhaps you should address the men."

"I will, briefly. We have a battle to win."

As Thalanius predicted, there was an outcry of outrage from some of the men when they learned of my decision to free the hostages, but I used the same argument I had with Thalanius, and many of the protestors backed down, though a few regarded me with mutinous stares. The hostages, meanwhile, could not believe their good fortune. They came and knelt before me, thanking me for my generosity. One even went so far as to say he would try to dissuade the General from attacking us. That got a good laugh from my men who heard him.

"Save your breath," I told him. "And possibly your life. Even his own son could not make him listen to reason. Go now, and thank the gods you live to fight today."

They did not leave entirely unscathed, as their departure was greeted by cries of derision and name calling from some of my soldiers, but that was a small price to pay for freedom. Thalanius and the other senior officers then gathered in my tent to go over our plan of battle. The Romans were disadvantaged by the hill they had to climb in order to engage us, but that would not give us much of an edge once they gained the summit. Their sheer force of numbers could then overwhelm us.

"We must make sure we stop them before they get this far," I said. "Make sure our archers are well armed and prepared. The more we kill or disable on the slopes, the better our chances are to hold them off. Once they are thrown into confusion, Thalanius and I will lead a cavalry charge on both their flanks at the same time. Then it's up to the foot soldiers, their downhill charge must shake the Romans enough in order that they retreat. Do not, I repeat, do not let your men follow. Tempting though it is, they must regroup and hold their position. The Romans will not give up easily. If they see our men scattered, it will give their cavalry the chance to defeat us."

"What if they send in the cavalry first?" Castes asked.

"That is not their way. They save the best for last. We must be prepared for that, that is why Thalanius and I will stay to hold their cavalry when they attack." Grunts and nods of assent greeted my words. "Then," I said, buckling on my sword belt, "if we are in accord, let us show the Romans our Gallic strength."

✱ ✱ ✱ ✱ ✱

LUCIUS

Flavius had assigned me to the cohort he commanded, but so far back I could only just see the plume of his helmet as he rode at the head of his troops. In front, were hundreds of infantrymen. I began to feel that even in the heat of battle I would be far from the action. I knew Flavius had done this to protect me. I had argued with him over it, but he had finally barked out an order I could not refuse without being seen as flagrantly disobedient, and worthy of the scourge on my back.

So, there I was, trudging along in the midst of hundreds of like armed and armored men, some of them joking and talking as if we were going on a picnic, rather than to fight a fierce and determined foe.

Of course, my mind was filled with thoughts of Callistus and our too-brief time for lovemaking. How I wished he had let me stay in the guise of a hostage, even though I knew that his first thoughts had been for my safety. Amazing, how little he had changed. Still the noble and beautiful warrior, despite the hardships and battles he had endured, during both his time with Spartacus and since his return to his homeland. The wound I remembered tending when he had come to me after the last battle under Spartacus was now but a faint scar across his lower back. One of many that covered his body, but in my eyes, far from detracting from his beauty, they only enhanced his physical appeal.

As ever, even when lost in the throes of passion, he had been gentle in his lovemaking, holding me with a tenderness that filled my heart with so much love for him, I could scarcely breathe. It had been more than three years since last I had been in his arms, and yet it had felt so familiar, so right...

A commotion ahead of us tore me from my reverie. Had we been attacked? I wondered. But, if so, where were the cries of battle, and the clashing of weapons? Then came a hubbub close by as word was spread through the ranks; the hostages had been set free! All of them had been returned unharmed, by order of the prince himself! I smiled a secret smile. Of course he would not harm them. It was beneath him to soil his hands with the deaths of those who, in the end, could not really harm him. Add nineteen men to a force of thousands, and what difference did it make? He would have sent them back with the order to fight well, that was his way.

The sun was at its zenith as we approached the foot of the hill we had to climb in order to engage the Gauls. There we paused, awaiting further orders. Some of the men crouched down on their haunches, others lay on their backs, resting after the long march and before the rigorous climb ahead of us. *Was it only yesterday,* I thought, *that I had ridden up that same hill to deliver the General's message to Callistus?* Now, staring up to where I could vaguely make out the front line of Gallic troops, I narrowed my eyes to see if I could distinguish his tall, fair-haired form among their numbers. I could not. Suddenly the air was alive with a thrumming, whistling sound I could not at first identify. It was followed by screams of pain and bellows of rage.

Arrows. Hundreds of them, descending on our troops in the vanguard of the force. I watched, appalled, as the sky darkened under a second barrage of the deadly barbs. Panic and confusion swept through the ranks. Centurions, riding up and down our flanks, yelled at us to hold fast. Then we were ordered forward at a brisk trot. This is it, I thought, the moment of truth for all of us. Who will die today, and which of us will survive?

We ran, heads up, eyes trained on the enemy that now I could plainly see holding their position, calmly waiting for us. Then, out of nowhere it seemed, came galloping horses and the spine-chilling cries of the warriors astride them, speeding down upon us, swords and axes slashing and ripping at flesh and bone.

All around me, men fell in a welter of carnage. A blow to my helmet sent me spinning backward, tripping over fallen bodies, and sprawling in a helpless pile on the ground. Dazed, I tried to get to my feet, but my legs would not obey me. I stared up as two men, a Roman and a Gaul, fought to the death over me. The Gaul, big and heavy, stumbled over my feet, giving the Roman an advantage he quickly took. With a downward slash, he all but severed the Gaul's head from his body. The Gaul toppled over, landing on top of me, winding me completely. I lay there, unable to move, the prodigious weight of the dead man kept me pinned to the ground. A kick to my head from a sandaled foot dazed me even more. I became disoriented, and lay there staring up at the sky and listening to the sounds of the battle that raged on around me, until a blessed unconsciousness overcame me, and I knew no more.

Flavius

The Gaul's cavalry had taken us totally by surprise. There had been no sign of any mounted force reported by our scouts, damn them all to Hades. If we survived this day, they surely would not! Ahead of my cohort, the main attacking force had faltered under the deadly barrage of arrows. The gaps in the line were not being filled quickly enough from behind. I ordered my men forward at the run, and that's when the Gauls surprised us.

I saw Prince Callistus lead the first cavalry charge. Bare-chested, his flaxen hair streaming in the wind, he looked like an avenging god as he raced at the head of his men, charging straight into our ranks, his sword wreaking havoc among the troops. Trying to rally my men was near impossible. Attacked from both sides, they panicked, bumping into one another in an effort to escape the flailing hooves and slashing swords that gouged a great path of destruction through their ranks. Fortunately, reinforcements in the form of another cohort arrived, and we managed to regain the ground we had lost. The Gallic cavalry attacking on our right flank was beaten back, but the prince's headlong charge had proved more effective, cutting off part of my cohort from the main body, and leaving them weak and easy prey.

I heard the order to retreat, and urged my men to fall back. Surprisingly, the Gauls did not give chase, but regrouped behind Prince Callistus and his cavalry. But we were not home free. The sound of their deadly arrows once more filled the air, striking fear into the hearts of those who fled from the field.

× × × × ×

Callistus

The men cheered as they watched the Romans flee. The day was ours, and with few of our number lost. The Roman dead lay in heaps upon the ground, most of them taken by our first onslaught from the archers. I gave the order to search for any of our dead or wounded among the Romans, lest any should be left behind without proper burial or care. Leaving the men to celebrate their victory, I urged Belenus forward and rode slowly along the edge of the mound of bodies lying atop one another in grotesque parodies of pale and bloody lovers. I shuddered as I imagined Lucius lying among them, and prayed to the gods that he was far from this place of death. I watched as several of my men, carrying stretchers, searched for anyone still alive— and then the impossible happened. I heard a low moan, and the scrabbling of what seemed to be someone trying to free himself. I dismounted and drew my knife, walking toward the noises. I heard a curse, in Latin, and drew in a quick breath of surprise. I knew that voice!

"Lucius," I whispered.

His head, covered in blood, appeared from beneath a body. "Callistus," he groaned, falling back again. I pulled the dead man from him, and gasped at the sight of his body soaked with blood. I slipped my arm under his head and lifted him slightly.

"You were victorious?" he asked in a murmur.

"Yes," I replied. "Your wounds are severe. Don't try to move."

He shook his head, and to my surprise, managed a smile. "Not my blood, just a blow to the head. Knocked me out..." He grasped my arm as he noticed the knife in my hand. "Are you going to kill me?"

"Not today," I replied, smiling into his beautiful dark eyes. "But I am at a loss to know what to do with you."

"I am your willing prisoner."

"We took no prisoners, Lucius."

"Oh..."

I unbuckled his breastplate and threw it to one side, then lifted him into my arms and stood up, calling for a stretcher bearer. With a sigh, he laid his head on my chest and nuzzled my right nipple with his lips. Even standing there, on a battlefield littered with the dead, his touch could still arouse me to desire. The two men who hurried to my side were more than a little surprised to see me holding a Roman soldier in my arms.

"Take this prisoner to my tent," I told them, disregarding their curious stares as I laid Lucius on the stretcher.

"Shall we fetch the surgeon?" one asked.

"Not yet. There are others more severely wounded who need his attention."

I mounted Belenus and accompanied the men as they trotted toward our encampment. My gaze remained fixed on Lucius, while my mind tried to find a way to keep him with me. He had been fortunate this day, only a minor head wound, but the Romans would be back very soon, intent on our defeat, and Lucius, were he to report back to his camp, would be forced to march against us again.

No one seemed to notice that I had taken him to my tent. The men were celebrating their victory, and until I called for Thalanius, he would most likely be similarly occupied. But at some point I was going to have to explain Lucius' presence, and why I had not simply disposed of him. The men knew of my compassion, and tolerated it, though they did not understand it, and given our situation would understand it even less when they found out I was harboring an enemy soldier in their midst. Once we were alone, I examined his head and was relieved to find it was mostly bruising.

"Take off your tunic," I said. "I'll find you something else to wear till we clean off the blood."

He nodded and stripped off the blood-soaked garment. At the sight of his sleek, lithe body it was all I could do not to pull him into my arms and ravish him on the spot. He smiled as he recognized the glint in my eye, and pressed his naked body to me, wrapping my arms about him.

"I know this is not a good idea," he murmured, "but the sight of you always fills me with the need to feel your flesh on mine. Can I be blamed for wanting you so much?"

"Only if I share the blame," I replied, kissing his sweet lips. "But now is not a good time, Lucius. The stretcher bearers will have already passed on the news that I have Roman soldier in my quarters. Thalanius will no doubt guess that it is you, but will wonder why I have brought you here."

"Is it not possible that we were friends before all this?" he asked.

"That is what I will tell him, that you were the mediator that Lentullus called for when there was rioting in the *ludo*, and that I had a deep respect for you then, and still do." I kissed him again. "And not one word of that is untrue."

"Oh, Callistus..." He clung to me, his lips on mine. "Know that I love you with all my heart, and always will, no matter what befalls us." His kiss was long, and filled with a yearning I shared, and wished to fulfill, but just then other matters had to take precedence. I handed him a tunic of mine and told him dress. "If Thalanius and Castes come here, leave all explanations to me." He nodded his acceptance, and sat on my bed to await my return.

FLAVIUS

My father was beside himself with rage as he berated me, and all his other officers, for the defeat we had suffered at the hands of the Gauls. His blame included everyone, save himself. He had listened, he said, to the advice of those who considered themselves seasoned campaigners, who had fought the Gauls before, and who had assured him they were no match for Roman superiority. In some aspects, his tirade was justified. The Gauls had taken us by surprise—that was their strength. Our greater numbers had been quickly whittled down to give them the advantage, but my father was also to blame for not deploying more men in the first place, and for not sending reinforcements when it was obvious we were in dire straits.

It took Tribune Egnatius, in his usual blunt way, to point this out, and to suffer the brunt of my father's rage as he turned on him in a most unseemly display of vicious insults. The other officers gasped as he sent forth a stream of vindictive slander, upbraiding him for everything, from being an arrogant and self-important boor, to an unpopular leader whose men would rather piss on him than follow him into battle.

All this, Egnatius took with a small smile of disdain on his face. Perhaps he was arrogant and could be full of his own importance, but he was loved by his men, something of which, right now, my father could not boast.

"General Sedonius," Egnatius said, after my father had depleted himself of any further invectives, "I must agree that we were at fault today, however, the fault lies squarely at everyone's door, yours included. You are our commander; we look to you for leadership, for strategy, and for victory. It will go in my report that all of those elements were missing from you as our commander."

"You would dare? Your insults border on mutiny, Egnatius. I could have you executed for this!"

"I think not," Egnatius drawled. "Your officers are in agreement with me—even your own son is in accord with us. I would now ask that you step down as commander, and hand over your authority to me."

I thought my father's head would explode. He stared at Egnatius, speechless with rage, his face almost black from the pent up fury that now blazed from his eyes. It was obvious he now regarded all of us as his enemies. Then amazingly, he drew his sword.

"You will not usurp my authority," he hissed, spittle flying from his lips. "Guards," he bellowed. "Arrest these men—all of them," he added, giving me an especially lethal look.

But Egnatius had primed the guards beforehand, and instead of arresting us they disarmed my father, then stood awaiting further orders.

"You are confined to your quarters, General," Egnatius told him, with some relish. "Tomorrow we will launch another attack on the Gauls. You will remain here, under guard."

"You cannot do this!" my father screeched.

"But we have just done it, Sedonius. Don't worry," Egnatius smiled, enjoying the moment. "When we are victorious, your shame will seem less. Come gentlemen – we'll use my quarters for further planning on tomorrow's battle."

"Flavius..." My father's groan caught at my heart, but I could not now withdraw my support for Egnatius. I looked at him, sympathy in my eyes, but then turned and followed the others as they filed out of the tent. I knew he would never forgive me for what I had done, but in my heart I also knew that it was for the good of the campaign. If we were to win in the morrow, against as brilliant a foe as Prince Callistus, we needed a man who was a strong and decisive leader. Unfortunately, my father was not that man.

CHAPTER IX

LUCIUS

I waited nervously for Callistus to return with Thalanius, his second in command, the man who had suggested that he should send only my head back to General Sedonius. When the tent flap was flung back, and the fierce looking, bearded warrior strode in, I feared the worst. Then I noticed he was a little unsteady on his feet. Thalanius had been celebrating a tad too merrily by the looks of things! I rose to greet him.

"So, the Roman pup has returned," he slurred, staring at me through narrowed eyes. "This time we *will* send his head back to Sedonius!" He then laughed uproariously while Callistus winked at me.

"I have explained to Thalanius that I found you on the battlefield, Lucius," he said, putting a hand on his friend's shoulder to steady him. "I also explained that because you showed me friendship and tried to bring compromise between Spartacus and the *ludo* owner, before the slave rebellion, I could not just leave you there to die."

"And you're not really Roman are you?" Thalanius asked over a hiccup.

"I am from Capua," I replied, thinking he'd probably never heard of it. "But we give allegiance to Rome, when we have to."

"Hmm, maybe you should fight them instead. Allegiance to Rome... never!" He smacked Callistus on the back. "Eh, my Prince? Death before we bow the knee to Rome!"

Callistus gripped his hand and held him close. "Aye, Thalanius, death, before slaves to Rome!"

I shivered as I heard them utter that oath. Death was so near us now at all times, and oh, how I yearned to take Callistus away from all of this. To ride with him to a far country where the name of Rome had never yet been heard, and to live our lives together, until we grew old. He was looking at me, a sad smile touching his lips, and I could tell he knew my thoughts.

Thalanius gave me a bleary-eyed stare. "Well, young pup, be glad that our prince is a man of compassion, and has a long memory. You'll be safe enough here, I'll see to it."

He turned to go, but Callistus stayed him with a hand on his arm. "Make sure the sentries are alert. Have the scouts bring back news of any Roman preparations. Any sign of battle readiness, and I'll want to know immediately."

"Yes, my prince."

"He's a good man," Callistus said, after Thalanius had left us.

"Yes," I moved into his arms and laid my head on his bare chest. Just then, I was content to feel the warmth of his embrace, and listen to the steady beating of his heart. He tilted my head and kissed my lips. "I love you," I murmured.

"And I love you, my Lucius. Come," he said, after kissing me again. "The men will celebrate well into the night. Let me show you one of my secret pleasures."

He led me outside to where Belenus was tethered, and with little effort lifted me into the saddle. He mounted behind me, and we set off at a canter, leaving the campfires and the sounds of revelry behind us. The moon was bright, lighting our way across the moor toward where I could see the outline of some tall trees. I didn't know where we were headed, nor did I care. All I wanted was right here, the man whose chest I now leaned back upon, whose arms enfolded me, and whose lips sent shivers of delight through me as he gently nibbled at my earlobe.

Belenus whinnied softly as we entered the shadows of the tall trees, picking his way carefully over the soft mossy ground. After a while, I thought I could hear the sound of rushing water. Callistus reined Belenus in and dismounted, tying his reins to a tree branch. I slipped off the horse's back and stood looking around expectantly. He took my hand and led me through the trees. The sound of water got louder, and I smiled with delight as we entered a rock-laden grotto, over which a waterfall tumbled and splashed its way into a pool. It looked almost too perfect to be a random act of nature.

"Did the gods plan this?" I asked, slightly in awe of the beauty before me.

"Perhaps," he answered, drawing me close. "The water comes from the mountains beyond us, mostly underground until it reaches these rocks, then spills into this pool. There is another underground channel that prevents the water from flooding the land around it. Come, I'll show you."

He stripped off his tunic, leggings, and boots, then dove head first into the water. Tugging off the tunic he'd given me, I followed. Below the surface of the water, he gripped my arm and together we swam to the bottom of the pool, where he pointed to a narrow opening between some fallen rocks. I nodded my understanding, then he pulled me into his arms and we rose to the surface, our naked bodies locked together as one. He turned onto his back, and held me as we floated on the surface of the pool. I felt as if I were dreaming. *How could this be real?* I wondered. Just Callistus and I in this almost surreal place, gazing up at the stars, lost to the eyes of the rest of the world. Such bliss could not be imagined, and I wished for it never to end.

"What are you thinking?" he asked in a whisper.

"Of how much I love you," I replied, "and of how much I long for a life that holds only you and I."

He held me close as we reached the shallow end and we could stand, sheltered by a wall of rocks that formed a smaller pool. He kissed me, a hard and hungry kiss that spoke of his passion and desire, and I clung to him, returning that kiss with a hunger equal to his own. He lifted me into his arms and climbed up onto the mossy bank, where he lowered me to the ground, then lay over me, his magnificent body covering mine completely. His kisses were filled with an ardor that set every fiber in my body alive with desire. I wrapped my arms and legs about him, pressing myself to him as if I could fuse our skin and flesh together. There was no closeness close enough; no kiss that lasted long enough. In my craving to have him here with me forever, I prayed to the gods to make time stand still, and for us never to leave one another's side.

"Let me taste you," I whispered. He moved over me, bringing his cock to my lips. I teased at the head with my tongue, letting the juice flow and gathered its salty sweetness in my mouth. I voiced my appreciation with a sigh of satisfaction, then sucked in as much of the hard, throbbing flesh as I could. He let out a long groan, caressing my face, stroking my hair, all the while slowly pumping his manhood past my lips. My hands roamed over his body, sliding up the sides of his torso, fondling his nipples, bringing them to small stiff points. I teased them between my fingers and thumbs, inducing gasps of pleasure from him. I felt his cock spasm in my mouth and I knew that he was close. I lifted my head, taking him in all the way to the root, the head of his cock now lodged deep in my throat.

A long guttural cry escaped his lips as he came, his semen pouring from him, choking me with its force. I clung to him, holding him locked to me until every spasm had ceased and every drop of his seed had been drained from him. Only then did I ease back, letting my tongue slide over his still-sensitive cock head as he slipped from between my lips. He gazed down at me, and my heart leaped in my chest at the sight of his beautiful face caught in the rapture of love. Truly, there was nothing more that I could ask the gods for. That look told me that he held me as dear as I did him, and I was content. He eased himself down the length of my body 'til his still-rigid cock was nestled between my thighs. His lips on mine, his tongue sweetly caressed the inside of my mouth, bringing me rapture. I wound my arms and legs around him, his hand grasped my aching erection and I slowly pumped in and out of his fist.

"Callistus," I moaned against his mouth.

"Yes, my beloved," he whispered. "Let me taste the sweetness of your seed." And as I gasped out a warning of my imminent climax, he lowered his head and took my cock in his mouth. I cried out his name again as I filled his mouth with my semen and my body shuddered in his arms with great, gut-wrenching spasms that almost made me black out. I clung to him, my face buried in his flaxen hair, the scent of sex and his maleness filling my nostrils.

"Sweet Lucius," he murmured, holding me tight against his body.

"My prince," I whispered, my lips pressed to the shell of his ear. "I love you."

✖ ✖ ✖ ✖ ✖

We dismounted outside his tent, where he tethered Belenus then said to me, "I will be back presently. I just want to ensure the sentries are alert."

I nodded and stood by Belenus, watching him stride away, my heart so overwhelmed with what had passed between us that had the world ended at that moment, I would have been content. This had been even more that I had ever hoped for. A sudden glint of metal in the darkness that surrounded me made me start. What…? A clink of armor came to my ears, soft, yet unmistakable.

Soldiers… I stood stock still, my eyes straining into the black night. Yes, a movement on the edge of the camp. Slowly, without looking left or right, I walked away in the direction Callistus had taken only moments before. I had to warn him, the camp was surrounded, I was sure of it. An attack was imminent. I wanted to shout out a warning, but thought it best I find him first. Where were the sentries? Why had they not sounded the alarm? Ahead I could see his tall figure suddenly frozen into immobility. I knew then that he had sensed what I had seen.

But, oh Jupiter, he was unarmed!

"Callistus!" I could no longer suppress my fear. "Soldiers… alarm, alarm!"

From everywhere, it seemed, there erupted a roaring of voices, the clash of weapons, and torches blazing in the night. I was surrounded by hundreds of men, fighting, slashing, screaming, cursing—and all I could think of was to reach him. To know he was safe, unharmed. But in the melee that engulfed me I could not see him. I was hurled to the ground and trod upon. Bodies rolled over me, stomped on me as I tried to get to my feet. I dodged a sword thrust, and attempted to run, but the press of bodies was too much to break through. Now I was fighting for my very life. I picked up a fallen gladius with which to defend myself, yet I did not know who my enemy was. I was out of uniform, unrecognizable to the Roman soldiers, but I could not harm any one of them, nor could I harm a Gaul. Crazed, I searched the heaving mob for a sign of his tall figure, of his fair hair. I screamed out, "Callistus!" but it seemed that in the chaos that surrounded us, we were lost to one another.

Then a rough hand grabbed me and spun me around. A fierce black bearded face scowled at me. "Thalanius," I gasped. "Have you seen him?"

"He's in the thick of it, of course."

"But he was unarmed!"

"Not anymore." He gripped me by the throat. "Did you betray us?"

"No! I would never betray him."

Whatever he would have said next died on his lips as a Roman sword pierced his side. For what seemed an eternity, he stared into my eyes, and then with a soft gasping sound, he fell at my feet.

The soldier who had killed him grabbed my arm. "Were you their prisoner?" It was Marius, a fellow recruit. I nodded dully, looking down at the man who had been loved by Callistus. "Come on then," Marius yelled. "We've got them on the run."

Because there was nothing left for me to do, I followed him and the Roman cohort as they pursued the fleeing Gauls. I was filled with a horrible guilt, and knew that Callistus, if he still lived, would be sharing that same remorse. Had he not taken me from the camp, he would be thinking, had he not let down his vigilance to indulge himself with me, this defeat might never have happened. The Gauls had been over confident, celebrating too hard, letting down their guard despite Callistus warning Thalanius to keep alert.

Over the heads of the soldiers in front of me, I could see the Gauls climbing a steep hill. No doubt they were going to regroup there, hoping to have the advantage of the higher ground, but to me it looked like it would prove a futile attempt. They had lost so many men, evidenced by the countless bodies that lay strewn under our feet as we ran in pursuit of them.

And then, in a heart-stopping moment, I saw him. At the top of the hill, he stood, rallying his men around him. My first instinct was to run to him, but then sanity took hold, and I stayed where I was, among the men I fought alongside. The command to halt rang out, and we waited while the leading cohort formed a long line that encompassed the entire foot of the hill. We were ordered forward. I felt out of place without my uniform and helmet, but as the men around me surged forward, I followed, keeping in step with Marius. We were marching up the hill; engagement with the Gauls was only minutes away. I began praying to all the gods to keep him safe, and that when the Gauls were finally defeated, his life would at least be spared. I knew that he would never surrender. They would either have to kill him, or take him captive by a force too great for him to resist.

I shuddered as I heard the Gallic war paean roar out from hundreds of throats. It was a roar of defiance, but also of desperation from men who knew that they could not win, but would die rather than be subjugated by a foreign power. What few archers remained within his army sent out arrow after arrow into our ranks, and every now and then I would hear screams of pain as they found their marks. But it was nothing like the bombardment we had encountered earlier, and fell short of throwing our army into the chaos of the previous battle. Onward we climbed, the vanguard finally clashing with the Gauls. There was a great surge of movement around me, and we were running into battle, and only the gods knew how it would end.

✷ ✷ ✷ ✷ ✷

FLAVIUS

I was but a few yards from the Gallic front line when it happened. Damn him, but he had done it again, was my first thought as the thunder of hooves heralded a cavalry attack on our flanks. At the same time he led his men into our center, gouging a great breach in our front ranks. As our soldiers rushed to contain it, they were cut down by the furious onslaught of the Gaul's headlong charge.

And then I realized that there was no cavalry, only riderless horses plunging among the men. It was a wonderful diversionary tactic—and it almost succeeded. His problem was, he just did not have enough men. Once we had grasped the fact that we were not being attacked by his cavalry, we could concentrate on routing the Gauls, who had by now fought their way so far into the center of our force that there was no escape. One by one they were cut down, until to my eyes it became a massacre. I rode into the midst of my men, shouting for them to stand down.

I reined my horse up in front of Callistus. He stood there, his naked body covered in sweat, and the blood of the men he had slain, his blue eyes blazing with defiance.

"Do not ask me to surrender, Tribune Sedonius," he rasped at me. "There will be no captives taken for you to chain and humiliate this night."

A low rumble of assent came from the throats of his men, who gathered more tightly around him. I found myself wishing that the men under my command were as in love with me as his men were with him. Every single one of them would gladly die for him, and of whom among my ranks could I say that?

"I will not humiliate you, or your men, Prince Callistus," I said, for all to hear. "Surrender now, and you will have spared the lives of your men."

He looked up into my eyes, and smiled. "I know you, Tribune, and I believe *you*, but your commanders, and your Senate, would say otherwise. Let us finish it now, in glory!"

As one, he and his men surged forward, and to my horror my men fell back under the attack. For a brief time, it looked as if he and his small band would rout a Roman cohort, so ferocious was their onslaught. And then the unimaginable happened. I gasped as I saw, as if in a nightmare, he and Lucius come face to face. It was as if the world had slowed, as if the sounds and sights around me had diminished, and I was only able to focus on the two men who now stood facing one another, swords raised to strike, yet hanging motionless in their hands.

"No!"

Was it I who had cried out? Just then I was not sure, but the vision cleared, and the world went back to encompass the chaos that surrounded us. I could no longer see Callistus, but I could see Lucius. He was kneeling over a fallen, flaxen-haired Gaul, and my heart hammered against my ribs as I dismounted and ran to his side.

"Lucius…" I put my hand on his shoulder, and his tear-filled eyes stared at me without recognition.

"I killed him," he sobbed. "I killed him… he would not strike, and left himself open to attack. I killed him…"

"*You* did this?"

He looked up at me as if I were a madman. "No! But because of me, he let down his guard…"

I looked down at his inert body, at the blood that seeped from the wound in his chest, and I said, loud enough only that Lucius could hear me, "He is not dead. His blood would not flow if he were dead. Staunch the wound with whatever you can find… your tunic… here," I pulled off the tourniquet about my neck and handed it to him. "Do it quickly, I will keep the men away from him."

I stood and surveyed the scene before me. Only a few Gauls, perhaps a dozen or so, remained alive. A centurion was barking orders, I left him to it and turned my attention again to Lucius. I knelt by him as he pressed my tourniquet to the wound on his lover's chest. Callistus was conscious, and gripped my hand in his.

"Do not let them take me prisoner, Flavius," he whispered. "Better I die here, than that." His eyes went to Lucius. "You must go, there is great danger for you if they see you here tending to me…"

"I will not leave you," he said, shaking his head. "Because of me, you were wounded…"

"Because of me, you are on this battlefield. Because of me, you joined this army…"

I sighed with impatience. "Stop with these self-recriminations. We must devise a way of getting you both away from here." I looked up at the clouds gathering across the face of the moon. "While the troops collect our dead and wounded in the dark, they will be too busy to bother us. If I help you up, do you think you can mount my horse?"

"My men…"

"All dead," I lied. If he knew that any were prisoners he would move heaven and earth to free them. Let him find out once he was safe. He could hate me then.

Lucius gave me a guarded look, then put his arm under Callistus to help him to his feet. I went to help him. The Gaul was heavy. His body, even in suffering, was all powerful muscle and sinew. Between us, we managed to get him on the horse, and I told Lucius to get up behind him.

"Belenus," Callistus gasped.

"His horse," Lucius explained. "He's tethered in the camp."

"If anyone challenges us, say nothing," I told them. "You are my prisoners."

"Won't they be suspicious that we are not headed toward the Roman encampment?" Lucius asked.

"I'll think of something to allay their suspicion," I muttered, grabbing the reins and urging my horse forward. As I had hoped, the darkness was our ally, and we were able to reach the Gaul's now-deserted camp without being stopped. Lucius jumped down to untether the fine steed that pawed the ground at our approach. He spoke to the animal in a low voice and stroked its muzzle, before handing me the reins.

"His saddle is in the tent." He ran inside and appeared a moment later, carrying the saddle and a long cloak. I saddled the horse while he wrapped the cloak around Callistus.

"There is a place where he will be safe, if no one follows."

"How do you know this?"

"He took me there, before the battle. Perhaps if I had not been here…"

"Lucius," I snapped. "Stop talking of ifs and perhaps. What is done, is done. Now we must find this place you spoke of, and bind his wound. I will try to bring some salve to stop an infection. But if, for whatever reason I cannot, let him rest a day or so, then have him guide you to his stronghold. There they can tend his wound properly."

He nodded and fell silent, climbing back up behind Callistus. The Gaul sighed and rested his broad back on Lucius' chest. We set off toward the trees that lay a short distance from the camp. After a mile or two of traveling through the dense forest, he said, "There, just beyond those taller trees, ahead to the rocks."

"You must have an excellent sense of direction," I remarked, looking around the grotto. "I only hope I can find it again."

I helped him ease Callistus from the horse and lay him by the pool. "Wash the wound," I told him, "then bind it. You'll have to use the hem of your tunic."

"It's dirty," he said doubtfully.

"Then wash it, too." I gripped his hand. "Lucius, I *will* try to return."

He brushed my cheek with his lips. "Thank you, Flavius. You have put yourself in danger for us. I will never forget your goodness."

"Nor I…" His voice was weak, yet Callistus managed a small smile through his pain. "The gods go with you, Flavius."

"And with you, *my prince*."

I mounted my horse, and left them there, all the while wondering just why I had acted so spontaneously to save him and Lucius. Callistus was a man of honor, he had proven that to me, over and over, in his actions and deeds during the time I was his hostage. Lucius I loved much as I would a brother. But I think it was more that I had seen their obvious love for one another—a love that had lasted, despite the distance and years separating them. A love I envied, and truly doubted I would ever find.

LUCIUS

After Flavius had gone, I stripped off the tunic Callistus had given me and dipped it in the water, rubbing it as hard as I could to wash away the dirt and blood. I could feel his eyes upon me as I knelt by the pool. I turned and smiled at him, and his lips moved as he tried to return it.

"I'm so very tired, Lucius," he murmured.

"You've lost a lot of blood," I said. "You must not move now the bleeding has stopped." I lifted the tourniquet gently to look at his wound. It was a vicious gash and deep, but the blood had congealed, stopping the blood flow for the moment. It needed stitching... Thorns, I thought, remembering how my mother had once sutured a cut on my arm when I was a boy. It had been painful, and was only a small cut, while this wound would require long thorns and many of them. I had no doubt Callistus would suffer in silence, but could I stomach the act of pushing the thorns through his flesh?

I tore a strip off the tunic and carefully washed away the sweat and dirt from around the gash. Blood oozed from it. I looked around for a suitable bush, and saw several briars growing at the base of the trees. Nasty traps for unwary small animals, but their thorns were long and sharp, and perfect for the job at hand. I broke several off, pricking my fingers in the process—they were sharp all right!

"Callistus…" He opened his eyes, and I showed him the thorns. "I could suture the wound with these, if you can stand the pain caused by my clumsy, shaking hands."

"Do it then, I promise not to scream too loudly."

I kissed his lips. Even at a time like this he could make light of the danger he faced. I cleaned the thorns as best I could, then, pinching the lips of the wound together, I thrust one thorn through. His eyes widened, but no sound escaped his lips. I, on the other hand, winced enough for us both. But I continued, pausing only now and then to wipe the nervous sweat from my forehead. When I finished, I wiped away the blood and heaved a long, shaky sigh of relief.

"Did I hurt you?" I asked, brushing his lips with mine.

"Yes." He grasped my hand in his and squeezed. "But I thank you." He looked up into my eyes. "I worry that if you are found here with me, they will punish you severely."

"They would execute me," I said. "But I doubt if they will come looking for you. Flavius will no doubt say that he saw you killed in the battle. We will stay here until you can travel, then I will take you to your home. That's what Flavius instructed me to do. There you will get proper care and rest."

He closed his eyes again, the effort of talking to me tiring him. I covered him with his cloak and sat by his side, holding his hand, glad that he could sleep despite the burning pain in his chest. As I gazed down on his noble face and magnificent body, I prayed to the gods.

To Jupiter, the god of war, that he might save this brave warrior; to Juno, Mistress of all the gods, that she would give us safe passage, and to Venus, the goddess of love, that she would bless us with a future that we could share with one another. She, I invoked with even more ardor, for I knew now that I could not live without Callistus. I was sure he would survive his wound, and I could even foresee us reaching his home—but then, his standing among his people, and my being a soldier in the Roman army, would surely be obstacles too great to overcome.

I could not just give him up, and deep within me, I harbored the hope that he felt the same. I knew he loved me, but did he love me enough? He loved his people, his country, they were everything to him; his reasons, for so many years, to fight and to live—and just where did I fit in? I sighed, for only he could answer that question, and I dreaded the day when I would have to ask it.

He muttered in his sleep, it sounded like, *Lucius,* or was I being fanciful? I rose and removed the saddle from Belenus, who had been contentedly munching on leaves and small branches. In one of the saddlebags I found one of his under garments and slipped it on. I lay down beside Callistus, holding his hand and pressing my lips to his neck. Sleep, take me, I thought, and in the morrow, let him be well.

✖ ✖ ✖ ✖ ✖

But in the morrow, he had a fever. I awoke to his ramblings, his sweating body soaking mine. I jumped to my feet and dunked my tunic in the cool water, then laid it over him. I rinsed out Flavius' tourniquet and held it to his lips. He licked at it greedily, so I cupped my hands, filled them with water, and let him lap at the water. Exhausted, his head fell back and he looked up at me, his usually brilliant blue eyes now cloudy and blank.

"Callistus," I whispered. "It's Lucius, I am here with you." I peeled back the binding over his wound, and gasped with dismay as I saw the inflammation around it. Almost instinctively I pulled out one of the thorns, and gagged as yellow pus mingled with blood poured out. Had I done wrong in closing the wound? I wondered, desperately. It had seemed the right thing to do, but then, I was not a physician. Perhaps the thorns caused the inflammation… I dabbed at the wound with a wet cloth, wiping up the mess that had slowed to a trickle. Was that a good sign?

A rustling sound from the trees made me jump up and grab the sword Flavius had left me.

"Lucius, it's me, Flavius." He led his horse into the clearing, and frowned with alarm on seeing Callistus' obvious distress. "What has happened?"

"He has a fever, and the wound is poisoned I think," I said. "Thank you for coming back," I added, as he knelt by Callistus' side and touched his burning forehead. "The wound oozed pus, but it seems to have stopped."

He peered at the suturing work. "You did this?"

I nodded. "Did I do wrong?"

"I have no idea, but I brought some salve from the physician." He grinned at me briefly. "I told him I had a cut in a place I did not want him touching." He rummaged in his pack, and brought out a small pot which he handed to me. "It should be applied three times daily. I also brought you some clothing, and some food and wine."

"Flavius, I can't thank you enough," I said as I smeared the salve over the wound.

"Thank me when you are far from here. Send me a message one day telling me that you and he are ensconced in some happy land together."

"If there were only such a place," I murmured. "What news from our side?"

He smiled wryly. "You still think of it that way? Well, my father is still confined to quarters, screaming about mutineers. Egnatius has declared himself commander, and the men seem loyal enough. I told them I had seen Callistus felled in battle, and indeed two or three others swore they had seen him fall, too."

"Will they advance into Gaul?"

"No. The numbers of dead and wounded are too high, and Egnatius thinks the Senate will not send reinforcements for some time, a new campaign perhaps, next year."

"Next year," I repeated.

"Yes, Lucius, time for you and Callistus to be far from harm."

"He will never leave his people." I put a clean piece of my tunic over the wound, and stroked his brow tenderly. "He loves this land and his people more than life itself."

"But perhaps not more than you."

"I would never ask him to put me before all else, Flavius. When he is strong again, whatever he decides, I will abide by."

He smiled and touched my face with his fingertips. "One day, I would wish to have a love like yours."

"And I will pray that your wish is granted, Flavius. You have been a true friend."

"Thank him for making me see beyond the here and now," he said. "The time I spent as his hostage was something I will never forget—nor regret." He pushed himself to his feet. "I must go before I am missed."

I stood and embraced him. "The gods protect you, Flavius," I murmured.

He kissed my lips and neck, and held me close. "And you, sweet Lucius." Then, with one last look at Callistus, who made no movement, he swung up onto his horse and was gone.

✖ ✖ ✖ ✖ ✖

Callistus slept for most of the day. Of this I was glad, thinking that rest would promote healing, and less suffering from the fever. What now? I wondered. What lay ahead of us looked bleak, but I would try to remain optimistic until Callistus had recovered his strength, and we could talk of our best plan of action. Occasionally, I would mount Belenus and cautiously patrol the woods around the grotto. It seemed to me to be a prudent move, for there was no telling what strangers or vagabonds might stumble upon us by accident. I kept these sorties short in case he awoke while I was gone. Toward evening, when I returned from one such patrol, he seemed restless. I placed my hand over his brow and felt a lurch of hope in my heart. The fever was abating, his breathing was calm and steady, and when I looked at the wound it had not become inflamed again.

He opened his eyes, and this time they seemed alert and focused. "Lucius," he murmured. He lifted his hand and touched my cheek, then he struggled to sit up. I put my arm around him to give him support.

"Rest," I urged. "The fever grows less, but you must not overtax yourself. Are you hungry?"

He nodded, and I reached for the bread and cheese Flavius had brought us. "Flavius came back," I said, "and brought us food, and salve for your wound. He told me the army will not press on into the interior. Their losses have been too great."

His eyes held a sadness I found hard to bear. I knew that he would forever hold himself responsible for the lost lives of the men who had followed him. I sat with my arm supporting him while he ate a little of the bread and cheese, and drank some watered wine.

"Flavius is a good man," he said, his voice subdued and heavy.

"He loves you," I told him. "Loves and respects you."

"He loves us both. In another life, perhaps we can be friends again." He laid his head on my shoulder. "This is not what I envisioned for my people. This defeat puts thousands in jeopardy."

"Flavius said it was unlikely there would be another campaign until next year. Will that give you enough time to raise another army?"

"Perhaps, but unless I can convince the other tribes to join as one, we will not be able to stop the Roman armies indefinitely." He shifted restlessly. "Tomorrow we must leave here."

"But you're not ready to travel," I protested. "The wound is still open, Callistus. Each step will cause you pain."

He peeled back my makeshift dressing and peered at his wound. To me it looked grotesque, a livid gash run through with barbs, but he merely grunted. "I've had worse," he said. "The gods were merciful. The thrust could have been through my heart."

I shuddered at the thought, and at the way it had happened. "There would be no wound if I hadn't been in the way. I swear, Callistus, when we came face to face, my heart stopped. It was as if all my nightmares had become one. Everything I ever dreaded was manifested in that one moment when you stood over me poised to strike, until you recognized me."

"And then, of course, I could not strike," he said. "Believe me Lucius, this is a small price I pay for having you by my side. If I had killed you, I would have deemed my life worthless."

He touched his lips to mine, and the emotion he had invoked in me with his words was almost his undoing. Just in time, I prevented myself from gathering him in my arms and crushing him to me with all my strength.

"Oh, Callistus," I murmured, capturing his lips gently with mine. "Every fiber in my body yearns to make love to you with all the passion we have shared before. But know this, when you are healed, you and I will have a consummation that the gods in their heavens will envy!"

He tried to chuckle, but the pain in the effort made him grimace instead. "Then, my sweet Lucius," he said, recovering quickly. "Speed me to my home, and those who can heal me!"

CHAPTER X

We left our safe place a day later, his ears deaf to my entreaties that we stay until he was stronger. I understood the urgency he felt to be home, his uncle, the king, would as yet be unaware of the defeat his countrymen had suffered at the hands of the Roman army. It was up to him, Prince Callistus, to be the bearer of this terrible news, and to explain how it came to be.

I also knew the awful guilt he still felt. I could have made him listen to my rhetoric, to my rationalizing all that had gone before, but to what avail? He alone would bear the responsibility of the defeat, after all, he was the lone survivor... or so he thought. I had not told him that Flavius had lied when he said all the men were lost. For what would it serve? The men were now prisoners of Rome, and might as well be lost. Soon they would be fodder to appease the hunger of the Roman crowds in the arena. There would be no sign of the compassion Callistus had shown the Roman prisoners.

We traveled three days to reach the stronghold he called home. A formidable structure it was, perched high on a hill and surrounded by rough and rocky terrain. At night we had rested for only a few, too-short hours, and yet as we neared his home, he seemed to regain much of his strength. I marveled at his recovery, indeed, it was I who was much the worse for wear as we approached the stronghold. I had contracted a chill, and felt weak and out of sorts for the remainder of the journey.

The people came out to greet him as we came within reach of the stronghold's massive walls. They called blessings on him, and stared at me with inquisitive, but not unfriendly eyes. Inside the walls, we were met by the king himself, Banthius, to whom I was introduced by Callistus as "Lucius, the man who saved my life." More explanations would obviously come later. While Callistus was led away so that his wound could be treated, I was shown to a sleeping room, and immediately asked that a bath be drawn. Never had I felt quite so rank in my entire life. Even my journey to find Callistus in the camp of Spartacus all those years ago had not left me feeling quite so filthy.

The menservants who delivered the bath and hot water bore no resemblance to their counterparts who served in Roman households. There was no subservience in their demeanor, nor were they afraid to look at me directly. One of them, a sturdy young fellow with rufus-red hair and twinkling blue eyes, even tried to engage me in conversation. Though his Latin was terrible, I could just about make out that his name was Bactimius, and that he was cousin to Callistus. I expressed my surprise that he would be asked to do menial tasks like this, but he grinned and explained that more or less everyone did just about anything when necessary.

"I fight in next battle," he said proudly. "Callistus show me how to use sword."

At least that's what I thought he said, but he couldn't be more than twelve or thirteen, I mused. He stayed while I threw away the rag I'd been wearing and slipped into the tub. Heaven could not have been more welcoming than this, and I closed my eyes as the hot water soothed and relaxed my tired muscles. I wondered how Callistus was faring. No doubt the physician was staring in horror at the makeshift job I'd done with the thorns.

"You will fight with us?" The youngster's voice interrupted my thoughts. I opened my eyes, startled for the moment. I'd forgotten he was in the room.

I shook my head, no. "Prince Callistus has no need of me in his army."

"He needs every man!" Bactimius exclaimed. "I tell him you fight with us."

I grinned at his enthusiasm, and tried to picture the look on Callistus' face when he was given that order. I closed my eyes again and sank beneath the surface of the water. Bactimius seemed to take the hint, for when I came up for air, he had gone. Off, no doubt, to tell Callistus to recruit me at once. From my haven of warm water, I looked about the room that was to be mine for the foreseeable future. It was Spartan in the extreme: unfinished stone walls and flooring, furnished with thread bare rugs, a wooden framed bed, a chest and a chair. No luxury here, only the basics needed for a simple, uncluttered life.

When the water started to cool, I reluctantly stepped out of the tub and dried myself with a thin scrap of towel. A fresh tunic and sandals had been laid out for me, and I slipped on the tunic gratefully. The room was chill, so I took the bed cover and wrapped it around me in the form of a toga, then I sat in the chair and waited patiently for someone to come and take me to Callistus.

Instead, he came to me. Standing framed in the doorway, he looked so much like his old self that for a moment I forgot just how much he had been through in the past few days. His hair shone with health and cleanliness, his face had lost its gaunt and pain-filled look, and he was dressed, not in ostentatious finery, but in a dark blue tunic and cloak, which on him took on a princely splendor.

"Callistus," I murmured. "You look well…"

"Thanks to you." He crossed the room and took me in his arms. "The physician said, crude as your suturing was, it was undoubtedly the best thing you could have done." He kissed me tenderly. "Thank you again for looking after me."

"He dressed the wound properly?" I asked.

He nodded, peeling down the neck of his tunic so I could see. "He clipped the ends of the thorns, but left them there. He prepared a salve made from herbs and moss that he must change for me every two days. It feels better already. Now come, my uncle has had a meal prepared for us. You must be famished."

"Callistus," I put my hand on his arm. "What is to become of me here?"

"You are an honored guest, Lucius, and under my protection. Do you think that I would allow anything less?"

"But do they know I am a deserter from the Roman army?"

"I have told my uncle all that happened, he is bereft, of course, at the loss of so many men. I also told him how you and Flavius saved my life, and of our meeting six years ago, before the Spartacus uprising. He is aware of who you are, and of what you mean to me."

I moved into the warmth of his embrace, careful not to press too hard against his chest. It seemed to me at that moment that my life had taken such a radical change of direction, that I could scarce comprehend it, yet I was with the man I had longed for, and that in itself was enough to allay my fears for the future. That, and the kisses he now showered on my face and lips, making me forget everything but his presence and my love for him.

King Banthius was old, and ailing. It would not be long, I thought, gazing at the old man's wrinkled visage, before the people looked to Callistus to take his place as their leader. Surely that must be foremost on the king's mind, and although he had not mentioned it, on Callistus' mind also. At the dinner table he presented me once more to the king, who smiled wearily at me and bade me sit. There were no other guests. This was not a celebratory dinner to welcome Callistus home, there was no cause for celebration However, it was evident that the old king was genuinely fond of his nephew, and was glad to see him home safe, and if not sound, at least on the road to full recovery.

The meal was simple fare, but well seasoned and cooked with care. I must admit that after army rations and the last few days of making do with stale bread and cheese, this meal seemed like the finest I had ever eaten. The king ate sparingly, but Callistus and I both made up for his lack of appetite. I enjoyed watching Callistus fairly wolf down his food, and the sight of him sucking the grease from each finger made me hard. At one point he caught me watching him, and gave me a lascivious wink, leaving me in no doubt that his thoughts were as mine.

King Banthius pushed away his still-laden plate and drained his goblet, calling for more wine. "So, you are sure the Romans will not invade again, Callistus?" he asked, holding up his goblet for the servant to refill. "Why do you suppose they are willing to give up the advantage they now have?"

"Their losses were heavy, Uncle," Callistus replied. "And according to a reliable source the Senate was unwilling to pledge reinforcements so late in the year. In the spring, perhaps, we will hear of another army advancing on our borders."

Banthius looked at me. "And so it goes on, never ending, it seems. But for me, the end comes soon. For you, and for Callistus, the fight goes on." He fixed me with sharp eyes. "Whose side will you take in the next foray?"

Callistus cleared his throat. "We have not yet talked of that, Uncle…"

"But your loyalty lies where?" Banthius persisted, leaning over the table and staring at me with narrowed eyes.

"Uncle…" Callistus threw me a look of apology, but Banthius held up his hand to silence him.

"Better to know where a man's heart lies before you trust him too much, Callistus."

I locked eyes with the old man and said, "My heart belongs to Prince Callistus, Sire, therefore, if I am called upon to fight at his side, I shall do so."

"Even against your fellow Romans?"

"I am not Roman, Sire. I am Capuan, we are obliged to join the Roman army, but my loyalty, and my love, is for Prince Callistus."

"Love, you say." The old man chuckled. "Well, you will need that love to hold strong in the coming months, and beyond, I fear. Tell me, young Lucius, d'you love him enough to risk your life for him—and possibly die in the process?"

I nodded. "Yes, Sire."

"He has already proven to me that he is prepared to do just that, Uncle," Callistus interrupted. "What he endured to bring me home attests to his love and loyalty."

The king grunted, and threw back the last of his wine, then rose to his feet. Out of respect I jumped up, but he waved me back to my seat.

"I'm for bed," he said, yawning. "You youngsters can sit and talk all you want, but an old man needs his bed."

"Goodnight, Uncle." Callistus saw him to the door, an arm about his shoulder, until the attendants came to take him to his bedchamber. Callistus smiled at me. "He is impressed by you," he said.

"When he says 'love,' does he mean the word in the same way I do, I wonder?"

He grinned at me. "He is old, not stupid. He knows what is in our hearts, and while he will insist that I remarry one of these days, he is not about to forbid our love for one another."

I fell silent at the thought of Callistus with a wife. *Where would that put me?*

"Come," he said softly, as if he had read my thoughts. "What I would tell you is for your ears only. Bring the pitcher of wine to my room. We can talk there."

His room was only slightly larger that the one I had been given, and just as sparsely furnished. The bed was bigger, however, and covered with a quilt made of a brightly woven fabric. He saw me eyeing it.

"My mother wove it for me many years ago. I cannot bear to part with it, even though it has needed repair many times over."

"You mother, is she…?"

"She died some ten years ago giving birth to my baby sister, who also died. It was a year of harsh weather, and she had been sickly for some time."

"I am sorry."

He nodded, accepting my sympathy without words, then he pulled me into his arms. His wince made me pull back, but he brought my head to his shoulder and stroked my hair gently.

"You worry that when I marry, your place at my side will be made tenuous. Believe me, Lucius, that will never happen. I must marry, and sire an heir. I must be a husband to my wife, and a father to my son, but you will always have a place at my side, and in my heart."

"Then that is all I could ask for, my love," I said, kissing his neck. I wanted to make love to him, to hold his naked body pressed to mine, to let him feel my hunger for him. He sensed my need, for his hands were stripping away my tunic and he bowed his head to nuzzle my chest, worrying my nipples gently between his teeth.

"We can do some of this," he said gruffly. "My need is as great as yours. We have been too long apart to let a trifling wound still our passion for one another."

It was not a trifling wound, and I told myself to be careful as I removed his cloak and tunic. The right side of his chest had been skillfully wrapped, the binding anchored over his shoulder, so I concentrated on his left side, scouring his muscular torso with my lips and tongue, and bringing a long groan of pleasure from him. I sank to my knees, and for a moment or two was content simply to gaze up at him, silently adoring the man who, for so many years now, meant everything to me. His smile, and the lust that blazed from his eyes as they met mine, took my breath away. I stroked his thighs, then leaned in, licking the warm muscular flesh that led to that part of him that could still fill me with awe. His cock curved upward, the head glistening with the essence of his need, his balls heavy with unspent semen. I slid my tongue under them, along the silken path that led to his opening. As the tip of my tongue teased at his hole, his hands clutched at my hair, caressed my face, and he breathed my name in a long sigh.

"Lucius..."

I grasped the base of his cock and licked at the juice that spilled from the slit, before taking the long, thick shaft in my mouth. His body shuddered from the impact of my tongue swirling over the hot, hard flesh. I ran my free hand up over his buttocks, holding him locked to me while I sucked. His skin was slightly scented from the soap of his recent bath, but underneath it I could smell his maleness, and it inflamed me with the desire to have him inside me. I stood up and led him to his bed.

"Just lie there, my love," I whispered. "Let me pleasure you…"

As eager as I was to have him, I knew that rampant sex would tear his wound open, and I could not inflict that on him just for my own, and yes, for his need, too. I straddled his thighs, and went down on his still hard and throbbing cock, coating it with my saliva until it was slick and ready, and as eager as my anus was to receive its prodigious girth. I eased myself onto him while he caressed my chest, teasing at my nipples with his thumbs and forefingers, sending ripples of pleasure through me. I took him in slowly, savoring every magnificent inch of his cock, feeling it fill me and bring me an ecstasy beyond anything that had gone before. Each time I laid with him, it seemed to surpass the time before, if that were possible. I leaned forward to take his lips with mine, and the growl that rumbled from his chest as our lips met caused me to chuckle into his mouth.

"Do I please you, my prince?" I asked, teasing his lower lip gently with my teeth.

Instead of answering, he grasped the back of my head and held my mouth prisoner with his. His tongue swirled over mine, waves of sensation coursed through my entire body. My heart quickened, my blood seemed to flow faster, and my cock, pressed against his hard torso, throbbed with the need for release. I pulled myself upright, arching my body and bearing down on his rigid shaft. My need quickened my rhythm over him. He grasped my cock, pumping it with strong, steady strokes, bringing me to the brink. The fountain of semen that erupted from me splashed across his chest just as his body shuddered under me. The surge of his orgasm made him cry out hoarsely, and his pelvis bucked under me as he filled my entrails with the hot blast of his seed.

I collapsed over him, taking care not to press upon his wound. His arms held me fast, and I pressed myself to his side, my lips touching his shoulder. In the quiet moments after our lovemaking, I could so easily delude myself into thinking that all was well, and always would be.

× × × × ×

FLAVIUS

The messenger came as we were preparing to break camp and return to Rome.

"New orders," Egnatius told us after summoning all officers to his tent. "We are to remain here until reinforcements arrive—probably within the week. The Senate wants the Helvetii army destroyed once and for all."

"But they cannot know of the losses we've taken," I said. "The field hospital is full of badly wounded soldiers…"

"They will be sent back, of course, along with General Sedonius. The message says that the Senate wishes to take advantage of the army already in place, and the inroads we have made."

"Inroads!" One of the other officers snorted his derision. "We haven't gained one mile since we crossed the border. We're lucky to be alive."

Egnatius frowned. "Nevertheless, we have our orders." He looked at me askance. "You may wish to say goodbye to your father. He will join the troops being sent home. All of you…" His eyes slid from me to the other officers. "…Have your men prepare for a longer stay—and another battle. Once the Helvetii know we are advancing into their territory, they will send out troops to harass us."

I left them and made my way to my father's quarters. He was still under guard, though I would have deemed it unnecessary by now. My father was a defeated man; one who was aware of what had happened to him, but not the reasons why. He looked up at me dully as I entered his tent.

"Flavius," he muttered. "What news do you bring me?"

"We are to wait for the reinforcements now on their way, then we proceed to the Helvetii stronghold."

"Good, I want to be there when they bind that devil in chains, and whip him all the way to the steps of the Senate!"

"If you mean, Prince Callistus, Father, he is no longer a threat. He was killed in—"

"You have the body?" he interrupted, rising from his chair.

"His body was not found, but several men saw him fall in the battle."

"If his body was not found, then that devil did not die. I tell you, I shall be the one to bring him to Rome!"

"Father…" I cleared my throat before I continued. "You are to return to Rome with the wounded."

His face turned a dark red as he glared at me. "Under whose orders?"

"Commander Egnatius issued the order, Father."

"*Commander Egnatius,* that toad! That sycophantic pleb. I will see him executed for mutiny. Him, and all who stood behind him, and if that means you, my *son*, then so be it!" He turned away from me and waved a dismissive hand. "Go. I will tell your mother how proud you made me."

"Father, it is better this way…"

"Get out of my sight," he seethed. "I never wish to see you again. You are henceforth disinherited from all my wealth. Think on that, the next time you obey a mutineer!"

Of course I knew my mother would never allow such a thing as my disinheritance to actually happen, yet I was in despair as I left him. What, I wondered, would he think if he knew that I had been the one to help Callistus escape the battlefield? Perhaps then, he would deem execution too good for me!

CHAPTER XI

CALLISTUS

My scouts' reports were far from welcome. I had hoped for time to rebuild our army to its former strength by personally going to the other tribes for support. Now I would have to send messages of warning to them that the Romans were awaiting reinforcements before advancing further into Gaul. The Saquini were our nearest neighbors, and had a strong force of fighting men, but I had found them unreliable in the past, unwilling to take orders from an outsider. Still, in this hour of need, and with the threat as real to them as it was to my people, they might agree to rally under one banner. To the west were the Pictones, and it would be advantageous to have them cover our backs should we find ourselves hard pressed and having to regroup.

Our true advantage, however, was the location of the stronghold. The Romans were going to have to face rough terrain and steep rocks in order to reach us, and there were many places from which we could launch devastating ambushes. Without reinforcements, we were vastly outnumbered; surprise, therefore, had to be the main thrust of our defense. My uncle agreed, and we laid out plans as to where best it would be to position the men who would spring the surprise attacks.

I worried about Lucius in all of this. He had said he would fight at my side, and I did not doubt for a moment that he meant it sincerely—but when the moment came, and he was confronted by those with whom he had so recently served, would his resolve not falter? Frankly, I was loath to put him in a position where he had to choose, but knew he would be insulted if I asked him to stay behind and not fight. In the end, I decided it would be best if he made that decision himself.

The days since we returned to my home had, in many ways, been idyllic. Despite the circumstances that had brought us here, and the fact that we were on opposing sides, the bond between us had deepened and grown stronger. If some of the people thought his presence in their midst strange, they said nothing, at least not to me or my uncle. I think this was, in part, because of Lucius himself. He had already made friends with my young cousin, Bactimius, who followed him around, asking question after question about Rome, about the Roman army, about the young girls of Rome... all of which Lucius answered without tiring of being asked the same question over and over. It was easy to see why he had made such an excellent teacher. His patience was boundless.

As my wound healed, our lovemaking increased in strength and variety. He would peel the binding back, and blow on the now closed gash, and whisper, "Hurry up, so I can show my master how strong I really am."

"My master." I scolded him for using that term. "I am not your master, Lucius."

"Yes, you are, of my heart, and of my destiny."

Somehow those words made me shiver with apprehension, but then he would kiss me, and my mind would become blurred to all things except his presence, his warmth, and the sweetness his lips brought mine.

The day the Roman reinforcements arrived was the day we prepared for the unavoidable battle ahead. We deployed several units, spreading them out among the gullies and ravines that the Romans would have to traverse on their way to the stronghold. I had given orders that the main targets should be the officers—demoralizing the men by attempting to leave them leaderless. Not an easy task, for the high ranking officers would be well guarded. But the centurions, those who led small detachments of soldiers, and whose men looked to them for orders and encouragement, were the most important—and the most vulnerable. Our best archers were at the forefront, their arrows honed to points sharp enough to pierce a breastplate, shield or helmet.

It was not long, a matter of three days only, before news of the first sightings came in. "A vast army," the scouts said, bigger than anything the Romans had thrown against us before. Tens of thousands of men. I conferred with my uncle, and it was decided that the women and children should leave. The Saquini would give them shelter even if they did not send us reinforcements. I tried to persuade my uncle to go with them, but he refused. Old and weak of bone, he could still wield his sword, he said.

LUCIUS

I watched the preparations with mixed feelings of excitement and dread. In my heart, and because I knew the unrelenting might of Rome, I knew the Gauls could not win this war, but nothing could have persuaded me to tell Callistus that. He would fight to the end. I knew that, and I had decided that no matter what, I would fight by his side. Call me a traitor if you will, but I loved this man too much to ever desert him. For nigh on six years he had been the focus of my thoughts, my desires, and my love, and if it were to end now, it would fill me with pride, and love, to die defending him. Whatever the gods willed, so it would be.

He came to me in my room, the light of battle in his eyes, the fever of the warrior in his blood. We both knew at that moment that perhaps we would never be together like this again. The morning would bring death and destruction on both sides, would perhaps bring death to one, or both of us, but whatever the outcome, these next few hours were his and mine alone.

"Lucius..." He breathed my name on my lips as he held me fast, and I clung to him, melding our bodies as if I could fuse them into one being, one entity, never to be parted. We fell upon my bed, hands ripping away our clothing, pressing our naked bodies together, each one drowning in the touch, the feel, the scent, the taste of our flesh. His wound had healed, but the puckered scar was still livid against his golden skin. I kissed it gently and wrapped my arms about his neck.

"I love you," I murmured against his ear, and my heart soared as his arms tightened about me and I felt the hardness of his arousal throbbing between my legs. Just to know that I would once again have him inside me, to be joined as only two in love can be, was almost enough to satisfy me—almost. But the marvelous realization of it was infinitely better. It was as if neither of us could wait for that moment when he would enter me and once again claim me as his own.

I had prepared myself in advance, using a soothing salve to ease his penetration. I did not mind the pain it sometimes brought me, for the ecstasy that came after eliminated all memory of it. I wrapped my legs around his hips as he drove his cock into me with one long, smooth stroke. I held him fast in my arms, covering his neck and face with kisses as our bodies rocked together.

"I love you, Lucius," he gasped, and I felt his shaft pulse deep inside me. My heart swelled with happiness at his words while my body rose to meet his deep thrusts. We moved together in unison, every one of his downward strokes being met by the upward motion of my pelvis. He buried himself balls deep inside me and I wound myself around his torso, clinging to him with my arms and legs as though my life depended on it.

As his breathing grew harsh and his body stiffened in my arms, I tightened my embrace about him and showered his face and lips with burning hot kisses.

"Callistus," I murmured, "I do love you so. No matter what occurs, whatever lies in our future, my love for you will never fade."

"Oh, Lucius," he groaned, his entire being shuddering in the grip of a convulsive orgasm that sent his semen surging into me. Spasm after spasm jolted his body against mine, the sheer force and power of his climax bringing me to the brink. I buried my face in the hollow of his neck, my lips pressed to the heat of his skin, as I too came with unbridled ecstasy, spraying my seed over both our chests. He smiled as he ran a finger through it and brought it to his lips to savor.

Then he kissed me.

The following morning, I was roused from my bed by the sounds of voices in the hall outside. I recognized his voice above them all demanding order. Something was wrong. Quickly I slipped from the warmth and comfort of the bed and threw on my tunic and sandals. The door swung open and he strode into the room, his face grim and drawn.

"The Romans are but two leagues from here. They must have done a forced overnight march to get here so quickly."

"And the men you placed to slow them down?"

"They will hold them for a time, but my plan is to move part of the main force outside the gates to lure the Romans closer to the walls. Some of the men disagree, wanting to hold the Romans from the safety of the walls."

"That was the discord I heard outside?"

"Yes, but Lucius, I know the Roman strategy. They will lay siege to this place until we are starved out. Better to attempt a brief, if bloody battle, rather than a long drawn out campaign of monotony and despair."

I nodded, though I really did not know which was the better plan, never having been in a situation like this before. I only knew I would do as he bid me.

"And have you persuaded them?" I asked.

"For the most part, yes," He smiled ruefully. "Although my reputation has suffered somewhat as a result of the last defeat. They will not challenge me, this time, but if my plan fails, they may listen to those who urge different methods."

FLAVIUS

The Gauls hit us again and again as we marched toward their stronghold. The constant barrage of arrows and spears from their rocky hiding places was demoralizing, just as it was meant to be. We lost three centurions in the space of a half hour—it was obvious they were targeting the officers, to leave those soldiers under them leaderless and confused. The plan worked well, and it took considerable effort to get the shaken men back in line and marching again.

There was only one way to deal with this, and that was to beat the Gauls at their own game. I formed a small band of veteran soldiers, and together we peeled off from the rear of the column, climbing the steep rocks to take the Gauls by surprise from behind and above. It was to be a tough climb, so we left our heavy armor and helmets behind, arming ourselves with only swords and knives. We came upon the first group after only a few minutes. The gods were with us, for the Gauls, intent upon firing upon our troops below them, did not hear our approach until we had killed three of their number. The rest we dealt with in fierce hand-to-hand combat. I lost two of my men, but we overpowered the remaining Gauls with none escaping to give the alarm.

We scaled the rocks above us, and from this vantage point could see three more groups of armed Gauls waiting for our soldiers to come within range of their spears and arrows. Keeping low, close to the rocks, we were able to reach the nearest group of Gauls without being discovered. But here our good fortune ran out. As we sprang into action, a larger group we had not seen rounded the rocks ahead of us. We were cruelly outnumbered and my men were cut down in a matter of seconds, leaving me and the remaining soldiers no choice but to flee. Leaping over jagged rocks and boulders, we managed to escape from our pursuers, but only, I am sure, because they deemed it more important to stay where they were and further harass our troops. At least we were able to report the positions of the Gauls ahead of us. Egnatius decided on a different route that, though longer, took us out of range of the Gauls' deadly bowshots. Progress was slow, but sure, and soon the walls of the stronghold loomed before us, looking as impregnable as we had been told it was.

Not only impregnable, but also protected by a large force of men outside the walls. Callistus had obviously decided that a long siege was out of the question. We were to fight on his terms, and as if to give weight to my theory, I saw him sitting astride Belenus, at the head of his men. He gave us no time for strategy, his cavalry charging straight at our ranks before we'd had time to pause for breath. In seconds, we were caught up in the tumult of battle. Callistus and his horsemen breached our lines, their steeds crashing into our foot soldiers, sending them flying in all directions. Egnatius ordered our cavalry into action, and for a time they held the Gauls in check, long enough for us to regroup and strengthen our position.

I saw Callistus ordering his men back to the stronghold's walls, and Egnatius instructed the officers to lead our troops forward. We began an ordered steady march in tight formation toward where Callistus and his massed cavalry waited. Suddenly the air was filled with the dread sound of hundreds of arrows. Wave after wave of the deadly shafts shot from within the walls of the stronghold rained down upon us, causing chaos within the ranks. Despite their shields, the men were struck down, many dead, many more seriously injured. Callistus took advantage of our confusion and once more led another devastating charge that forced us to retreat. As my men ran for their lives, I was appalled to see them discard their shields and heavy spears, flinging them away in order to run faster from the pursuing Gauls.

I could hear Egnatius screaming out orders, but to no avail. We were routed, and all we could do was run, in the hope that we could regroup at some later stage. The rough terrain made our escape difficult. The sharp, loose rocks underfoot caused many men to slip and fall, unable to rise quick enough to escape a Gaul's spear or sword thrust. My horse was whinnying in fear as it scrambled over the treacherous ground, and only my gentle urging kept it from bolting in the wrong direction.

✖ ✖ ✖ ✖ ✖

Our defeat was unacceptable, Egnatius told we officers later, standing in his tent, listening to his words of fury as he vented his spleen upon our heads.

"Why were the men so easily routed? Where was the leadership they expected—and deserved? Where were all of you when they began to run? You should have been there rallying them, encouraging them to stand fast. Did you not hear my commands to fill the breaches and hold the enemy back?"

"Commander…" All eyes looked at me as I spoke. "The mistake was in not having the men rest. We should not have approached the stronghold as quickly as we did. Prince Callistus was relying on our eagerness to engage him, and he was well prepared for it."

Egnatius stared at me through narrowed eyes. "You're saying I am to blame for that debacle?"

I sighed. "No, Commander. What I am saying is that we are up against a clever foe, and we cannot disregard his strength, or his cunning. He can be beaten, but only by careful strategy. We cannot just plunge headlong into battle with him."

"But we outnumber the Gauls five to one," Egnatius seethed.

"We *did* outnumber them five to one," one of the other officers said in a disrespectful tone. "Now it's more like three to one."

"Our numbers mean nothing to Callistus," I interrupted. "His army is loyal to a man, and they are fighting for their very survival. If we outnumbered them ten to one, they would fight as long and as hard as they did today."

Egnatius said, "We will lay siege to his stronghold and starve him out. Let's see how loyal his men are when their bellies are empty. In the meantime, I will send word to Rome that we are in for a long campaign, and will need reinforcements."

"You think the Senate will approve of sending more troops this late in the year?"

"If they want the Gauls broken, then they will."

I left the meeting with a feeling of unease. Egnatius' new position as commander had inflated his ego and he was proving to be no better than my father at military strategy. It was going to take a much more able commander than either of them to defeat Callistus and his men. In my mind, he had the advantage. An almost impregnable fortress for protection, plus the ability to foray out and deal us shattering blows at will. Perhaps with the reinforcements, the Senate would also send a General worthy of the task ahead.

✖ ✖ ✖ ✖ ✖

LUCIUS

Callistus returned, the cheers of his men ringing in his ears. He had given the correct call and had been victorious. No one would question his ability to lead the Gallic forces now. He had not allowed me to accompany him outside the walls, but from that vantage point I had watched as he led his men to victory. When he came to me later, freshly bathed, his hair shining like a golden crown, his blue eyes still holding the glint of battle, he held me in his arms and kissed me with such fervor it would take an epic poem to describe the ecstasy to which he raised me during our lovemaking.

Suffice to say, his victory on the battlefield paled in comparison to the one he claimed upon my bed. An easy victory, you might say, and you'd be right. My resistance was poor and easily overcome, and I was all too ready to fall on my knees and make obeisance before my vanquisher. To the victor went the spoils, and it was with some self satisfaction that I deemed us both well rewarded.

Afterward, as we lay in the shelter of each other's arms, he told me of his scheme to avoid the lengthy siege the Romans were obviously planning.

"My scouts told me they sent for more reinforcements," he said, his hand gently stroking my chest. "I am surprised they are extending their campaign into the winter months. But the

Romans are nothing if not resolute. What I want to do is harass them as much as I can. Before they can become encamped outside our walls I intend to deal them some powerful setbacks that perhaps will make them want to abandon the siege and go home."

"But if there are reinforcements on the way…"

"The messengers were unsuccessful in their task."

"Oh,"

"I am counting on the fact that when General Sedonius returns to Rome he will accuse Egnatius of mutiny. The Senate will be obliged to recall Egnatius to face his accuser. If we can demoralize the army even further with our constant attacks, the other officers may just decide their best option is to go back with Egnatius. I have no doubt he will want some of them to support him when he faces the Senate's inquiry."

His reasoning was sound, I thought, and said so, and at the same time prayed to the gods that they be in agreement also.

"If all that happens as I foresee it," he continued, "it will give me time to ask the other tribes to rally to our side against the next invasion."

And so it would go on… I sighed, and he held me tighter in his arms. "You are troubled."

"Only because I see no end to this. When will you have time for anything other than winning battles? I am not a warrior, Callistus. I joined the Roman army for one purpose only, and in that short time I have seen so much death and destruction. So many innocent lives taken on both sides—and to what end? Will there never be peace, will we never see men and women living in accord with one another?"

"You have a gentle soul, Lucius, and if there were more minds like yours then perhaps peace would be possible. But as long as the need to conquer other people, and their lands, burns in the heart of the Roman Empire, no man is safe, and war is the only answer."

I knew he was right, yet I raged at the inevitability of war and conquest. How I longed to spirit us both away from it all.

To have him all to myself, without the fear of marauding armies and governments bent on killing him or taking him captive for later punishment. A futile dream, I knew, but one I yearned for with all my heart.

My fear for him made me groan with despair, and he raised himself on one elbow to gaze at me and stroke my cheek.

"You are afraid."

"Only for you. After all the years I have waited to see you again, I could not bear it if I were to lose you again."

"We must leave that to the gods."

"You said that to me once before."

"And they reunited us."

"Yes, they did—after exacting a high price."

"Everything of value has a price, Lucius."

I sighed. "And for you, it was a price I gladly paid, my love."

He lowered his head to mine, and took my lips in a tender kiss. "And a price I would pay again, and again," he whispered on my lips.

I held him while he slept after our second bout of lovemaking. Could I ever tell him that this was my secret delight? What better pleasure than to gaze at his face, smoothed by repose, to feel the warmth of his breath on my skin, and to gently trace his features with a fingertip, to softly kiss his eyelids, his lashes, his slightly parted lips. There was not a part of him that I did not love or ever tire of touching. Again, I thanked the gods for bringing us back together, and for giving us this precious time, even though it was still fraught with danger and uncertainty.

Whatever the future held for us, I knew our love for one another would be steadfast and true—even if he should take a wife. Somehow, I would find a way to deal with that occurrence, and I made a silent promise to him, that he would never see my face cloud with jealousy when he had to leave my side for hers. Besides, I told myself, kissing his chest then laying my head on his warm hard flesh, there is so much more to overcome before that day might become a reality.

On the morrow, he would begin the lightning raids in the hopes of discouraging the Roman army from prolonging their siege. I prayed that he would be successful.

* * * * *

Two weeks later

Flavius

I had never witnessed so much dissension among officers and men as I did in the days that followed our first defeat at the hands of Callistus and his army. Egnatius was determined that we continue to lay siege upon the Gallic stronghold, despite the setbacks we suffered on an almost daily basis. Each day and night brought a fresh attack; a lightning foray by the Gauls, burning our tents, destroying our catapults and storming platforms. Our men were jumpy and exhausted from nervous exhaustion and lack of sleep. The night raids were the most humiliating, as the Gauls could be in and out of our encampment in a flash, laying waste to anything in their path, and with hardly a man lost.

We, on the other hand, were counting the toll of dead and wounded on a daily basis—and we were sick of it. The men were becoming more and more vocal with their displeasure, and Egnatius had even been pelted with mud as he rode by a part of the barracks at dusk. He waited for reinforcements that I innately felt were not coming. By now my father would have reached Rome, and gone directly to the Senate to register a complaint against Egnatius. All I could hope for at this juncture was that the Senate would recall Egnatius to answer my father's accusations, and order our legions home. Winter was fast approaching, and I had no wish to be stuck outside in the freezing cold, with every shelter we built being burned to the ground.

Prince Callistus must be laughing at our plight, I thought time and again. And Lucius, what of him? Had he been accepted by the Gauls as a friend to their prince, or was he being held prisoner with even his lover unable to prevent his captivity? Despite our predicament, I found it in my heart to hope that he and Callistus were enjoying what they had earned—each other's love.

I had found companionship in the arms of a fellow tribune, Julius Catullus. He had come with the reinforcements that, much to my surprise, had duly arrived, and of course I had noticed him immediately. Taller than I, with wide shoulders, hair the color of russet brown and eyes so green it was hard to not stop and stare at them. He surprised me one night by asking me to join him for a cup of wine in his quarters. Of course I accepted, and as the night progressed we sat closer and closer together, until finally, almost impatiently, he kissed me.

My thoughts were interrupted by a summons to a meeting of all the officers. Could it be that at last Egnatius had seen the folly of our continued presence here?

He had the look of a defeated man as he stared at us from behind the table unusually devoid of maps or plans of strategy. His look of contempt for us seemed to linger upon my face longer than on anyone else's at the meeting. Outside the tent, I was constantly aware of the grumbling of the men as they made preparations for the night watch. The commander's eyes narrowed as he too, heard them.

"'Tis the sound of mutiny," he said in a growl. "The morale of the men has sunk to an all-time low, and I hold all of you responsible for that."

A ripple of dissent spread among the officers, but I remained silent. Too many times they had looked to me to voice their opinions, and all I had been rewarded with was Egnatius' scorn and their failure to support me.

"Silence," he roared. "An army is only as good as its officers. The men look to all of you for courage and direction—and right now they are getting neither."

"The men want to go home," someone said quietly.

"And admit defeat?" Egnatius snapped. "This is the Roman army, we don't give up so easily."

"There has been nothing easy about this campaign," I said, revoking my decision not to speak out. "I think it's time to face the fact that we are not in a position to maintain this siege. Winter is but a few weeks away. Any more of these raids will decimate our troops even further. Surely, Commander, you can see that without reinforcements and winter provisions, we are extremely vulnerable."

A heavy silence fell upon the group of men around me. All right, I thought, someone else speak up, or am I to be the only one again to make the point that we are wasting our time and men's lives here?

Then Julius, my newfound friend said, "Flavius is correct, Commander. The men become more frustrated and discontented every day. It might be wise to consider a withdrawal, and plan another campaign for the spring—*as was the original intention.*"

The deliberate inflection on his last few words sparked a fury in Egnatius' eyes. "You forget yourself, Tribune," he hissed. "Those decisions were reversed by order of the Senate!"

"Then perhaps the Senate should take over the siege, Commander," Julius said mildly.

I coughed my laughter into my hand, but Egnatius sprang to his feet, his face red with rage. "Insolence! I will not have this dissension within the ranks of my officers." His rant was interrupted by a cry from outside.

"Messenger approaching!"

By Jupiter, I thought, let it be what I have been praying for. I watched intently as Egnatius snatched the leather tube from the messenger's hand, pulled out the scroll and unfurled it. From the look of dismay and outrage on his face as he read, I knew he was being summoned back to Rome to face the charges of mutiny my father had told me he would level against him. Egnatius' eyes met mine in a cold stare.

"Dismissed," he rasped.

"But Commander, no decision has been reached," Julius said in protest.

"Dismissed!" Egnatius all but shrieked. "Except you, Tribune Sedonius, I need a word in private with you." He waited until the officers had filed out of his tent, then threw the scroll on the table in front of me. "You knew of this?"

"Of what?"

"Of this, your father's attempt to ruin my career—to blacken my name!"

"Was it not obvious to you that he would do so?" I asked him calmly. "Surely you didn't expect him to return to Rome and remain silent?"

"He is accusing me of *mutiny*, Flavius, mutiny. You were there, you saw how he was unfit to remain in command."

"Are we all instructed to return to face his charges?"

"No, just me…" He picked up the scroll again and glanced at it. "But we are under orders to withdraw from Gaul immediately. To terminate the campaign until the Senate decides on the next course of action. You and the other officers will receive further orders in due course." He looked at me, his expression suddenly hopeful. "I expect you to be a character witness for me when I face your father's charges."

"You can expect that I will tell the truth, Commander."

"I would ask nothing more of you."

I inclined my head, saluted him and left the tent. Julius was waiting for me a few yards away.

"Well?" he asked, falling step with me.

"He has been recalled to Rome to answer to charges of mutiny."

"And we have not?"

"No, but the siege is at an end."

"Thank the gods for that," he murmured, his hand grasping my bicep and steering me toward his tent. Once inside, he pulled me into his arms and kissed me roughly. "We must celebrate our good fortune."

I started to unfasten his breastplate. "And that may take all night," I told him with a smile.

"What will you do when we get back to Rome?" he asked, after kissing me again.

"My father is intent on disinheriting me. I have some money, so I will not be a vagabond on the streets."

He chuckled, his lips tickling mine. "No indeed. You will be a guest in my villa for as long as you wish."

All other words seemed pointless as our physical desire consumed us.

CHAPTER XII

LUCIUS

From atop a ridge among the hills, Callistus and I, mounted on our horses, watched the Roman army depart with a great deal of satisfaction.

Callistus turned to me and smiled. "See how they march, Lucius, as if they were the victors and not the vanquished. Roman arrogance knows no limits."

"What now?" I asked.

"They will return next year of course, with an even bigger army and larger siege weapons. Look, is that not Flavius at the head of his legion?"

I stared at where he pointed. "Yes, I believe it is him. I'm glad he survived the fighting."

"Yes, he is a good man—for a Roman."

We turned out horses away from the sight of the departing Romans and took a brisk canter over the hills toward the stronghold. The king had ordered a celebration to mark the end of the siege, and to honor Callistus, as well he should. It was my opinion that the old man should announce he was stepping down in favor of his nephew, and have Callistus crowned immediately.

When we returned, the king sent for Callistus and I went to my room to bathe. I had no sooner immersed myself in the warm water when young Bactimius, nephew to Callistus, came barging in without knocking.

"Have you heard?" he demanded, his homely face screwed up in disgust.

"I didn't hear a knock at my door," I replied tartly.

"Oh, that..." He waved a hand dismissively. "The Saquini have kidnapped our women!"

I sat up in alarm. "Kidnapped? But King Banthius sent them there for safety before the siege."

"That's right, and now they will not let them return. They are demanding payment for their safe passage home, otherwise they will be sold into slavery."

"A foolish move," I said. "Callistus will not let this go unpunished."

"The king has already ordered him to take a strong force and march against the Saquini."

I sighed and lay back in the tub. By the gods, I thought, can there not be a time when he and I can enjoy some time without the threat of war and violence? I looked to the door as Callistus entered.

"News travels fast," he said on seeing my glum expression. "Bactimius, you are fast becoming as great a gossip as any old woman."

"But this is news, not gossip," Bactimius protested.

"Go now, and let Lucius bathe in peace." He steered his nephew toward the door.

Bactimius dug his feet in. "You'll let me go with you, won't you, when you fight the Saquini?"

"If you go now, and leave us to talk." He closed the door behind the young boy, then turned to look at me. He was not smiling.

"Bad news," I ventured.

"Bad enough to cancel tonight's feast. It would not be fitting."

I nodded, then stood up in the tub. He handed me my towel, then lifted me out of the tub, holding my wet body pressed to his. I was soaking his tunic but he didn't seem to mind, so I did not resist.

"I must go and get the womenfolk back," he said, his lips against my neck.

"I know, I will come with you."

"No."

"Yes." I kissed his lips. "I cannot be left out of every fight because of your fear for my safety. I have seen conflict and I can use a sword. I am a man, Callistus."

"That I know full well. But this is not your fight."

"It is yours, therefore it is mine."

He sighed heavily. "I thought that, for a while at least, you and I would enjoy each other's company without the sound of battle echoing in our ears."

"Perhaps the Saquini will negotiate when they see you riding against them."

"I had not thought them so duplicitous," he said, rubbing the towel over my shoulders. "They have been our allies in years past."

"Men can have a change of allegiance."

"I had hoped they would ally with us against the next Roman campaign, but now it seems they cannot be trusted." He rubbed the towel over my hair, then cupped my face in his hands. "I could tie you to the bed before I leave."

I smiled into his eyes. "You could tie me to the bed every night, and I would not complain. But if you leave me behind, I will bellow so loudly the Saquini would hear me in their mountain fortresses."

He chuckled. "Perhaps it would serve as a diversion. I cannot dissuade you?"

"No." I kissed his lips, and held him there, my hand on his bare neck, under his flaxen hair. "I will be at your side in this."

"Oh, my sweet Lucius. Do I deserve this love you give me so unconditionally?"

"If that requires an answer, it is a resounding yes," I said, pressing my naked body to him. He lifted me into his arms and carried me to the bed.

"We leave for the Saquini border in an hour," he said, putting me down on the mattress and lying over me. His voice was husky with desire. "Enough time for me to show you how much I love you..." This time his kiss stifled any answer I might have given.

✖ ✖ ✖ ✖ ✖

The ride to the Saquini border was very much more arduous than I had anticipated. I had thought the terrain in Iberia to be truly treacherous for horse and man, but this wild country was beyond description. Never had I seen ravines as deep or mountain crags as high as these we passed through.

And people live here, I thought, taking a moment for a wary glance upward at the towering masses looming over our heads. I wondered if the Saquini were like their surroundings, wild and untamed—unpredictable and treacherous.

For two days we struggled on across this rugged land, strangely devoid of trees or any form of nourishing vegetation.

"Does nothing grow here?" I asked Callistus at one point.

"Once upon a time there were farms and villages here," he replied, his voice low and sad. "But the land has been laid to waste through countless wars between the tribes. It was always my hope that one day all Gallic tribes would unite under one banner, but it seems we have too many differences. And that, my Lucius, is our weakness."

The words of Flavius came to mind. On our first meeting at Venel Papni's house he had voiced that same opinion. If only the Gauls would unite, he'd said, they would be invincible. Why then, could they not see it also? Obviously Callistus understood it well. Perhaps one day he would be able to convince his fellow Gauls of the need for unification.

But it seemed that it would not be soon. Ahead of us, I could see mounted horsemen, armed to the teeth, waiting for our approach. Callistus flung up his arm, halting his cavalry and signaling his archers to the vanguard.

"They may wish to talk," he told me. "But just in case—" He was interrupted by a blood curdling yell, and the Saquini horsemen surged forward, thundering across the rocky ground toward us.

"Archers!" Callistus barked, his face set in a grim frown. "On my command, fire!"

A hail of arrows descended on the charging Saquini, bringing with them a chaos of screaming men and horses, of bodies plunging from their stricken mounts to be trampled under sharp hooves. I marveled at how, in the blink of an eye, havoc and disorder could suddenly fall upon even the most savage attack. The Saquini charge was halted well short of its intended target, and those of the enemy who still lived or could move fell back in confusion.

"Forward!"

Following his command we set off behind Callistus as he proceeded at a full gallop, signaling that his cavalry should encircle the Saquini and prevent their escape. I spurred my horse onward, trying to keep up with Callistus astride Belenus, but that steed had no equal that I had seen for speed and endurance. To my dismay, the gap between Callistus and the rest of us widened as he charged into the enemy ranks. My heart pounded with fear at the thought of him fighting alone, his back undefended.

But, as we came upon the enemy, I knew my fears were unfounded. Callistus had the Saquini commander at sword point, while his men struggled with one another to escape the Helvetiis' encirclement. Weapons were thrown down, and the Saquini stood silent and sullen as their commander surrendered to Callistus. I had learned only a few Gallic words and phrases, but they were enough to let me understand that the women and children entrusted to the care of the Saquini were unharmed. On hearing that, Callistus sheathed his sword, and bade the Saquini commander lead us to where they were being kept hostage.

CALLISTUS

The Saquini commander, Organatrix, was quick to tell me that he had been against the imprisonment of our women and children, and that he was only following orders. Of course, I did not believe him, and his lies only made me despise him more. The man was not to be trusted, and I made sure my men kept a sharp lookout for any treachery on the part of the men they guarded. We were led to an encampment about five miles from where the Saquini had hoped to stop us. It was poorly guarded, and when they saw our approach with their soldiers our captives, the guards threw down their weapons and surrendered immediately.

I was beginning to think that the Saquini would not have made able allies in our fight against the Romans. Quickly, we freed the women and children. Some were wives and families of the men who had ridden with me, and there was many a joyous reunion. I looked at Lucius, who sat astride his horse smiling at the relief and happiness on the faces of the women and children—and my heart twisted in my chest. He was not going to like what I had to tell him.

"Lucius, a word."

He spurred his horde to my side. "Yes, my prince?" He had insisted he address me in this manner in front of my people, even though I had told him it was not necessary. He had replied that it showed them he held me in deep respect, and had added, with a smile, that of course he did.

"Lucius, I want you to take the women and children back to their homes while I go on to meet with the Saquini king. I would like to impress upon him that this kind of villainy will not be tolerated."

"Then I must go with you!" he said, just as I knew he would.

"No, I am asking you to ensure that the women and children reach their homes safely."

"But any of your men can do that," He narrowed his eyes at me. "You are getting me out of the way, aren't you? You see possible danger, and you don't want me to face it with you."

"What I am asking you to do also holds possible danger, Lucius."

He shook his head. "No, twenty of your men will ensure their safety whether I am with them or not. My place is at your side. I will not have it any other way."

"You are refusing to obey a direct order?"

"Yes."

"Lucius," I hissed, under my breath. "Do not defy me in front of my men."

His eyes glistened as he stared at me. "It is not my intention to defy you, my prince, but you know only too well where my place is. I have sworn it, and it must be so."

I groaned. "Lucius…"

"Ask anything else of me, and I will obey, but do not ask me to leave your side in a time of crisis. I will not do it."

"I should have you sent back in chains."

His dark brown eyes sparkled with sudden mischief. "You seem to enjoy the prospect of tying me up, my prince," he said, his voice low and seductive. I felt my face flush and looked around quickly, but the men were too occupied with their womenfolk to pay us much more than passing interest.

"Your jest is inappropriate, Lucius," I snapped, and he chuckled to see me so discomfited. "I shall deal with you later."

I summoned some of the men, including my nephew Bactimius, and told them to form a column to conduct the women and children safely home. For a moment, Bactimius looked as if he too would argue my order, but a glare from me silenced him. Then, with the prisoners leading the way, I took the rest of my men, and reluctantly Lucius, into Saquini territory.

Word must have ahead that we had defeated the army sent to stop our progress, for we were greeted by an envoy from the Saquini king, asking that we would enter the city peacefully, and that the king would meet with us on the morrow. Until then, we would be his guests. My men would be quartered within the city walls and I would be conducted to lodgings as befitted my rank.

I told the envoy that the king's request was granted and that I looked forward to hearing his explanation for his hostile actions of holding our women and children hostage. The envoy nodded, ignoring my pointed remark, and conducted us into the city. While my men were shown where they were to bivouac, I signaled that Lucius should accompany me to my assigned lodgings. He grinned at me, no doubt recollecting my, "I shall deal with you later," threat of earlier. The thought of him and myself alone together for the evening sent a longing to my loins that made me shift with discomfort in Belenus' saddle.

The envoy, he did not say his name, guided us to a handsome house outside of which stood what I presumed to be the owners; an elderly man and a young woman, obviously his daughter. They bowed before me and ushered us indoors. The house was well built and spacious, with high beamed ceilings and an imposing fireplace in the main room.

"Prince Callistus, you are welcome here in my home." I was surprised that the young woman was the one to welcome me. "My father and I are honored."

"I thank you," I said. "And your names?"

"I am Dorcas, and this is my father, Urses." She paused and smiled. "You seem surprised that I am the spokesperson. My father lost the ability to speak after being wounded in a battle against the Romans—the same battle in which my husband was killed. This house was his."

"My condolences," I murmured. "This is my equerry, Lucius."

Dorcas lifted an eyebrow. "A Roman?"

"A Capuan," Lucius said, bowing slightly.

"And a soldier in my army," I added. "Now, if you would show us the room we will use…"

"Of course." Lifting the hem of her dress, she led us down a long and wide hall to another spacious room. "I am sorry, there is only one bed."

"That's all right," Lucius said, chuckling. "On campaign, the prince requires me to sleep on a pallet at the foot of his bed.

Perhaps you can furnish one?" I could hardly keep a straight face as Dorcas assured Lucius she would find one straight away.

"We will serve you dinner when you have bathed and rested," she said, turning to leave.

"My thanks." I watched her go, and then glared at Lucius. "On a pallet at the foot of my bed? Do you know what that makes me sound like?"

He laughed. "A prince who keeps his subjects in check?"

"A boor is more like it."

"Well, I could have said, 'One bed is sufficient, Lady. The prince and I share one frequently!'"

"Lucius," I growled. "Come here."

He closed the gap between us in a second and wound his arms about my neck. "Am I to be punished?"

"I cannot think of a punishment good enough for you," I said, kissing his nose.

"The only one that would break me is not having you in my life," he murmured, pressing himself to me.

"I told you that will never happen."

We kissed, and his lips on mine, as always, caused my heart to melt and the heat in my loins that started with his touch to become an unquenchable fire. We had to break apart and turn our backs to the door to hide our arousals as a loud knock came to our ears.

A beaming servant entered, pulling a large wooden tub into the room, and followed by more servants carrying pails of hot water.

The servant bowed and addressed Lucius, shielding his eyes from me. "Will the prince require a bath servant, sir?"

"No, that won't be necessary," Lucius said, trying to hide his amusement along with his erection. "I will attend the prince."

When the bath had been filled, and the servants gone, Lucius chuckled. "The Saquini are obviously more Romanized than they care to admit."

I nodded. "Yes, they were conquered and lived under Roman rule for many years. Their rebellion under the previous king was successful, but as you noticed, traces of Roman culture remain."

"Well…" He gave me a sunny smile. "I think we should take full advantage of it, and get in that bath, right now."

"We?" I tried to look displeased. "But you just dismissed the servants saying you would attend me."

"And attend you I will," he said, pulling at my tunic and kissing my chest as he laid it bare. "You and I, together in that bath. Could I be more attentive than that?"

I chuckled and crushed his willing body to mine. "Oh, my Lucius," I whispered, burying my face in the warmth of his neck. "You make each day of my life more bearable with your presence." I stripped him of his tunic and leggings, and together we climbed into the bath. He slipped behind me, rubbing the soap over my back and shoulders, massaging my muscles with his strong but gentle fingers. I leaned back against him, and his arms encircled me, his lips tracing a sensual pattern over my skin, his soapy hands stroking my chest, teasing my nipples.

I could feel his throbbing manhood pressing against my buttocks and suddenly I felt an overpowering need to let him claim me as I had him so many times before. No man before him had ever awakened this need in me. I turned my head to him, kissing his soft, warm lips, and whispered, "Lucius, my love…"

It was as if he had divined my need, for the kiss he returned, although still sweet and sensuous as always, now had a demanding edge to it—a demand I now gladly wished to fulfill. I turned so that I knelt before him in the bath, and gazed into his shining brown eyes that darkened with desire. I enfolded him in my arms and raised him from the water, bringing his erection to my lips. I took him into my mouth and held him there, my tongue weaving around his hard, sweet flesh. His body shuddered in my arms, his hands caressed my face, stroked my hair while he pumped his cock to a steady rhythm in and out of my mouth.

"Callistus…" He murmured my name, his voice husky with the need to take me, and I stood up, our eyes meeting with a complete understanding of what we both wanted. He moved into my arms and held me, his lips pressed to my neck. "I do love you so much," he whispered. I lifted him into my arms and stepped from the tub. The towels were within reach, and I wrapped one around him, but he removed it and began to dry me. I let him take charge, for this was what he wanted. He led me to the bed, pushing me gently forward so that I was bending over, face down. He knelt behind me and grasped my thighs. I shivered as I felt his warm, moist tongue lapping at the cleft between my buttocks. His hands moved to either side of my buttocks, parting them, his tongue probing at the entrance to my core. My back arched as ripples of arousal coursed through me. He plunged his tongue ever deeper inside me, past the circle of muscle that could resist him, but did not. The ecstasy he brought me was almost too much to bear, and I gasped as my cock spasmed and spilled its juices over my hand.

I felt a surge of anticipation as Lucius stood behind me, replacing his tongue with the head of his cock, and pushed his way slowly inside me. He was being so sweet, so gentle, thinking that as this was the first time any man had fucked me, I would resist, but the groan that escaped my lips was not from pain, but from impatience. I wanted all of him inside me. I wanted to feel the hot flesh of the man I loved fill me completely, take me, mark me, make me his own, for all time. Never before had I experienced these feelings, and I knew then that Lucius and I were to be as one—never more to be parted.

I pushed upward, drawing him deep inside me. I heard him gasp as his hands stroked and caressed my torso. I didn't care for the position we were in, I wanted to see his beautiful face when he came inside me. That transformation from lust to rapture as his orgasm overcame him. I moved away and turned over onto my back, pulling him into my arms and winding my legs about his hips. His cock found my waiting hole and he smiled down at me as he entered me again with one long, smooth stroke.

"Lucius, Lucius," I murmured, covering his face with kisses. His lips captured mine, his tongue plundering my mouth with a sensuousness that brought me to the brink so swiftly my breath caught in my chest. Intuitively sensing my beginning to lose control, Lucius quickened his thrusts; at the same time he gripped my pulsing erection in his hand and pumped it, matching the rhythm of his pelvis as he ploughed into me. Through love-filled eyes I gazed up at his face, now caught in the rictus of ecstasy as he neared his orgasm. A fine sheen of sweat coated his face and body. His lips parted, and a long visceral cry escaped from him as he came, his hot seed flooding into me, binding me to him for all time. I climaxed with him, the dizzying force of it causing my body to arch off the bed. I crushed him to me, holding him, kissing his face and neck with a fervor born from the intensity of our union.

As our blood cooled, he buried himself deeper in my embrace, and I knew he was, like myself, trying to prolong the sense of wonder that enveloped us. His cock was still hard inside me, and I shifted my hips slightly in order to keep him there. His breath and lips were warm against my neck, and as we lay there, locked in each other's arms, I made a silent vow that wherever life's path should take me, Lucius would always be an integral part of it.

Lucius

Nothing could have prepared me for the emotional onslaught that welled inside me following our lovemaking. That I loved Callistus with all my heart and soul was something I knew beyond any doubt. But this... this incredible sensation of being *inside* him, of feeling the silken heat of his core surrounding my throbbing flesh, was beyond anything I had ever experienced before in my life. And after, nestled in his arms, my heart still beating fast from the sweet passion of our mating, feelings of fulfillment and well-being washed over me, making me forget for the moment where we were, and why we were there.

Until now, I had thought that fighting alongside my warrior prince had been my most thrilling hour, but even that could not compare to the rapture he had just brought me. I wondered if the young king Alexander, who had conquered the world, had felt like this in the arms of his lover Hephaestion, or Patroclus in Achilles' embrace. But as they had all died untimely deaths, I didn't ponder upon them too long.

"What are you thinking about?"

His voice startled me for a moment, then I stretched like a contented cat in his arms and kissed his chest. "Of you, my prince," I replied. "And of how amazing my life has become."

His chuckle came from deep inside him. "You mean how dangerous it has become."

"That's true." I raised my head from his chest to grin at him. "But you know, from experience, that the threat of danger won't keep me from your side."

"You mean your *disobedience* won't keep you from my side."

"True again." I ran one hand down his side and poked him in the ribs. I had found out some years before that my brave warrior was ticklish. He jumped as I kept my finger there, and added a great deal of pressure.

"*Lucius…*"

Ignoring his warning tone, I began to tickle him unmercifully. As hard as he tried not to, choking laughter soon erupted from him, filling the room, and I'm sure the entire house as it increased in volume.

"Lucius!" he roared finally, grabbing my hands and pinning them to my sides. For a long moment he glared into my eyes, his expression a mixture of affection and exasperation, before wrapping me in his strong arms, effectively rendering me incapable of further attacks. Then his lips were on mine, and with a happy sigh I opened my mouth, letting his tongue slide in.

I could feel his hard cock throb against my belly. I slipped from his embrace and ran a trail of kisses from his mouth to his groin. His first murmur of protest became a deep sigh of contentment as I nuzzled at the head of his penis before taking it all into my mouth. His hands stroked my hair, and he uttered little growls of pleasure as I laved the underside of his cock with my tongue. I drenched his throbbing shaft with my saliva, then sat astride his hips, guiding his hot, hard flesh into my eager hole. As I slowly eased myself down the length and thickness of his pulsing cock, he pushed his pelvis upward, driving himself into me, filling me with the strength and power of his manhood. His hand gripped my aching erection, propelling me towards my climax.

"Callistus," I whispered, gazing into his brilliant blue eyes, now filled with a hunger that took my breath away. I fought to control the rushing in my blood, to prolong once more this moment of ecstasy, but as he drove his cock even deeper inside me I erupted, a stream of semen splattering across his chest and onto his lips. With a feral smile, he licked at my seed, and then one final buck of his hips and he came, his body arching upward as he pumped his hot essence into me. I collapsed on top of him, and again his arms imprisoned me against his hard, heaving chest. His lips took mine in a kiss that blurred my already weakened senses. We lay without movement for a long time, each content to simply bathe in the afterglow of our lovemaking.

When he stirred beneath me, I moaned in protest. He chuckled, and patted my bottom.

"I fear our hosts will send that servant again to tell us supper is ready—and we are not!"

"You're right," I said, kissing him quickly and rolling off him "Best make ourselves presentable at least." I tested the water in the tub, barely lukewarm, but enough to wash the signs of our recent activity from our skin. "Hurry," I told him. "Let me attend you in your bath!"

He laughed as I hastily dunked myself in the water, rubbing away the dried semen. He rose and padded toward me, and for the hundredth time at least I could not help but take pleasure at the sight of his magnificently sculpted body. The warrior incarnate, I thought, unable to control my leer.

"Lucius…" His smile belied his tone of reproof. "Surely even you are satisfied, for a little time at least." He climbed into the tub, and I made a pretense of being suitably offended.

"Was that a complaint, my prince?" I huffed, handing him the soap and stepping out of the tub to give his big body enough room.

"Not at all," he replied. "My complaint is directed at your lack of attention to my bathing needs."

"My prince, you know what will happen if I get back in there with you, and it was you who said our hosts will be expecting us presently."

"Well," he grumbled. "At the very least, you could wash my back."

"Give me the soap…"

He chuckled as I lathered his back and shoulders. "Not bad," he said. "With some training you might make a very good bath attendant."

Any tart reply I might have made was stilled as a loud knocking sounded at the door. I threw a towel around me, and opened the door just enough to see it was the servant who had brought us the bath.

"My mistress wishes to inform you that they await you in the dining room." His eyes took in the fact that I was undressed.

"We will be there presently," I said. "The prince wanted to rest before bathing."

"Does he require more hot water?"

"No, no. He is almost ready. A few minutes only…" Callistus was already out of the tub and drying himself as I closed the door.

"So, pleasure must give way to tedium," he said, reaching for his tunic and slipping it over his head.

"Perhaps they have a good wine to serve with the food."

He watched me for a moment as I strapped on my sandals, then when I stood up he took me in his arms and kissed my forehead.

"Thank you," he murmured. "You have made this day, which could have ended badly for all of us, into one of the happiest of my life. Sweet Lucius, if I do not say it enough, know that I treasure your company above all else—and that I love you more than I ever thought it possible to love anyone."

"Callistus, prince of my heart," I murmured. "I love you more than life itself."

His lips touched mine, gently at first, and then with a hungry and demanding passion that had us both writhing in each other's arms.

He pulled back, panting, a choking laugh on his lips. "Oh, my Lucius, as much as I hate the idea, we must go to dine with our hosts!"

CHAPTER XIII

LUCIUS

It was done quite skillfully. As we entered the dining room, Dorcas and her elderly father rose to greet us. She extended her hands to Callistus, who took them, and inclined his head slightly. Suddenly the room was full of armed soldiers. We were surrounded by about twenty men with drawn swords. Callistus and I were unarmed. Bad odds at the best of times.

Callistus looked around him, amusement touching his lips. "So many to subdue two unarmed men, Dorcas?"

"Your reputation as a warrior preceded you," she said, with a wry smile.

"But yours as a devious traitor did not," I retorted, my eyes fixed on hers. She bridled at first, but under my steady gaze she dropped her eyes and looked away.

"To whom have you sold us?" Callistus asked.

"The Roman Senate put a price on your head that our king could not ignore," the old man said.

"My men will not allow me to be taken."

One of the soldiers stepped forward. "Your men are our prisoners, Prince," he said gruffly.

Callistus stared at the man for a long moment. "I know you," he murmured. "We fought side by side against the Romans last year. You are named Argan. You would do this now? First our women and children, and now this? Have the Saquini lost all sense of honor?"

Argan stared at Callistus, obviously stunned that he would remember the name of a man briefly met in battle. He shifted uncomfortably. "Sire, I follow the king's orders."

Callistus nodded. "Even though you do not agree with them..." He gazed around the room, and then shrugged. "Very well, but I advise you this. Guard me and my men well, for should you falter, you will pay a price far greater than any ransom the Romans may reward you with."

We were led away, but not before I cast an evil look Dorcas' way. Her father, at least, had the grace to look ashamed. They took us to where the men were detained. By the looks of things the Helvetii soldiers had not succumbed easily. Several bodies, both Saquini and Helvetii, lay sprawled about, and when his men saw Callistus under guard, they raised a raucous cry of rage that had the Saquini soldiers backing away in fear. Callistus held up his hand to quiet them.

"It seems we are to be the guests of King Brennus for longer than we anticipated," he told them. "Make the best of it for now, until I can devise a means for our release."

One of his men stepped forward. "We could take them, Sire. The Saquini are cowards, depending on treachery to surprise us."

"True..." Callistus smiled at the man. "But right now they are armed, we are not. Don't worry, I will think of something. I'm not ready to visit Rome just yet!"

I shuddered as I thought of all the terrible torture and degradation they would heap on him in Rome. I had heard of captives being treated abominably as they were dragged in chains through the city streets, I could not bear to see him treated thus. Somehow, we must escape!

He gripped Argan by his arm. "Take this message to King Brennus: 'At least have the decency to meet with me face to face. To take an ally captive without explanation shows a lack of honor and kingship. Is this the legacy you wish to pass on to your sons?'"

Argan blanched. "Sire..."

"For the sake of our comradeship in battle, Argan, you will do this for me."

Argan nodded stiffly. "I will take your message to the king."

I watched Argan as he strode away, and the gates to the compound where we were held were slammed shut.

"Do you think the king will listen to your message?" I asked.

"He better," Callistus said grimly. "When news of this treachery reaches my uncle, he will send an army against Brennus. If he does not release us before then, this town will be laid to waste."

"Then why is he taking such a chance? There is no Roman army near to aid him—or does he know something we do not?"

"We saw the Romans leave, Lucius. An army that size cannot easily hide from sight. My scouts would have reported to me if the Romans had turned back."

I nodded, yet I felt uneasy. Why would King Brennus risk a hostile Helvetii army's wrath, if he had no reinforcements? Callistus sensed my doubts.

"There is only one other possible explanation," he said after a moment or two. "One of the other tribes may be in collusion with Brennus. They might think that their combined forces may be enough to stop us."

The words of Flavius came back to me. He had told me the Gaul's weakness was in their refusal to unite under one standard. But to deliberately antagonize the Helvetii into battle at a time when there were no Romans to pay the ransom for Callistus' capture seemed a foolish ploy. If they meant to keep him prisoner until the Romans returned, perhaps in the spring, that was even more foolish. Callistus' uncle would not stand idly by and see his nephew a prisoner for that length of time.

Callistus lowered his voice slightly as he continued. "I think the real reason Brennus wants to give me over to the Romans is not so much for the ransom, but rather to stop me taking over the leadership when my uncle either dies or considers himself too old to continue ruling. Brennus has long envied our more fertile land and the near invincibility of our stronghold."

"You mean he wants to merge the two tribes?"

"More likely he wants to destroy the Helvetii and resettle our land with his own people. He knows I would stop any such plan, so he has to rid himself of my threat."

I looked to the compound gate as it swung open and Argan approached us. "I relayed your message to the king, and he will grant you an audience immediately."

Callistus smiled grimly and gripped my arm. "My equerry will accompany me."

Argan nodded and proceeded to lead us from the compound. Callistus' men watched us leave with worried expressions. I could tell they did not trust the Saquini with the life of their leader, and no doubt wondered why he had not taken several of them to ensure his safety.

King Brennus was a large man, in girth and in bluster, but small in courage. Here were Callistus and I, unarmed, and on a mission of peace and good will, and Brennus had seen fit to surround himself with a small army of bodyguards in order to receive us. I say "us," but of course his business was with Callistus, and he did give me a queer look as I strode in by my prince's side.

"So, King Brennus..." Callistus did not bow, considering himself, and rightly so, of equal rank. "I find myself a prisoner, and you willing to sell me to the highest bidder. Is this the way a king treats a prince, and an ally?"

Brennus seemed at first lost for words, obviously not prepared for Callistus' straightforward approach.

"The Romans want to debase you, Callistus, for the humiliation you have poured on their heads. They threatened me and my family if I did not comply." he said tersely. "They put a price on your head, Callistus, to overcome my resistance to holding you hostage. I do not like what they have asked of me, but they assured me you would not be put to death..."

"What then," Callistus interrupted. "Am I to be a slave for the rest of my days? Better death than that!"

"They gave me no choice!"

"And so you are willing to carry out their orders," Callistus said. "Are the Saquini now the servants of Rome?"

Brennus had the grace to look ashamed. His face flushed and he looked away before answering. "As I said, they have threatened my family."

"You have an army," Callistus pointed out. "An army of young, strong men willing to defend their country against invaders. Are you about to allow them to become mere vassals to Rome? Will this be the legacy you leave your son, who must rule after you?"

"Enough!" Brennus glared at Callistus. "You seek to shame me, but it is you who are the captive, Callistus. You and your men will remain my prisoners until I receive further instructions."

"And after Rome has rewarded you, what then? You know as well as I that the Romans are never satisfied until they own everything. They may leave you on your throne, but you will be the ruler of nothing, Brennus. They will take your land, subjugate your people, inflict their culture, their gods and their philosophies upon you. The Saquini will become Romans—is that what you want?"

"I said enough, Callistus!" Brennus was shaking with either rage or humiliation, I could not be sure of which.

"All that your father succeeded in doing, you will undo with this act of treachery," Callistus said. "He at least wished his people to live as free Gauls, not as slaves to a corrupt empire!"

"Guards!" Brennus screamed. "Take him out of here. Throw him in the pen with the rest of his men. He no longer deserves my hospitality."

Callistus laughed. "Nor do I want it, Brennus." He put his arm around my shoulder. "Come, Lucius. Let us join the only brave men here—the Helvetii!"

❈ ❈ ❈ ❈ ❈

LUCIUS

For three days we were kept confined like animals by the Saquini. Callistus, I think, expected Brennus to have second thoughts of treating with the Romans, but as time went on and brought no word of our release, he became impatient and angry.

"By the gods, Lucius, we must break out of here before we die of hunger and disease," he rasped as yet another day of being exposed to the elements loomed before us. There was no shelter to be found in the pen, and the burning effect of the noon sun was taking its toll on the men's fair skin. Many had blisters across the faces, shoulders and arms. Callistus' skin was a fiery red and itched abominably. I was luckier than most, being used to long hot summers, but the lack of food and water was wearing me down.

"Before we are too weak to fight, I must get the men out of here," he said.

"What do you propose? I asked, dully.

"Something you may all hate me for until you are free," he said, getting to his feet and walking over to where the Saquini guards were stationed. What was he talking about? I wondered. What could he possibly do to make me, or any of his men, hate him? I watched as one of the guards trotted off, obviously about to convey a message from Callistus. A few minutes later and about ten guards descended on the pen, opening the gate and signaling for Callistus to accompany them.

"What's he doing?" one of the men asked.

I shook my head. "He did not tell me..." But I had an uneasy feeling in the pit of my stomach. Whatever he was planning, I could only hope that I would be by his side. He did not return that day or night, and in the morning when there was still no sign of him, the men grew restless and worried. An hour after sunrise, guards, carrying barrels of water, rations of bread and cheese, opened the gate and brought the water and food to us. Callistus had obviously come to some agreement with Brennus, but what could it be that would have the king relent and ease our punishment?

The rest of the day I festered, worrying about Callistus and missing his company terribly. We had not been apart from one another for several months, and his absence weighed on my mind, and my heart, like a heavy stone. That night with still no sign of him, I questioned one of the guards. My Gallic was still far from perfect, but it was enough to have him understand my concern.

"Your prince has deserted you," he said, sneering at me. "All of you. He left under guard this morning."

I felt my heart sink. "Left? But for where?"

"For Rome of course. He agreed to hand himself over peacefully if King Brennus would guarantee your release."

"Oh, no…" I turned away to face the other men who were gathering round me, their searching eyes already seeing from my expression that all was not well with their leader.

"He has given himself up in order to secure our release," I told them, the words bitter in my mouth.

A stunned silence followed my announcement, then one by one they raised their voices in protest—but I did not join them. I cared not that they were now leaderless, or that they would return to their homeland to vent their outrage to King Banthius. All I cared about was that Callistus had sacrificed himself for them—had left me, for them—and to be delivered into the hands of his mortal enemies from whom there surely could be no escape for him, this time. My grief descended on me like a black cloud. I found a corner of the pen and sat on the ground, burying my head in my hands, trying to block out the sights and sounds of the Helvetii soldiers as they shouted their outrage at the Saquini guards.

Once again, Callistus and I had been parted, and only the gods knew if I would ever see him again.

✻ ✻ ✻ ✻ ✻

Brennus waited a whole week before he released us. In truth, I was surprised that he did in fact release us. I had thought that a man with as few scruples as he would simply have had us all put to the sword as soon as he knew Callistus was safely in the hands of the Romans.

Argan informed us that a Roman convoy had met Callistus and the Saquini guards at the border and were now conveying him to Rome. By keeping us all here until that had been accomplished had made it impossible for us to mount a rescue attempt. What now, I wondered as we were herded out of the pen and set on the road back to the lands of the Helvetii. With Callistus gone, I had no desire to remain among the Gauls, friendly as they had been to me. I was sure that Bactimius, Callistus' nephew, would welcome me into his home, but that was of little comfort to me.

As we marched together over the rough terrain that lay before us, I knew that only one path was open to me. Return to Rome and help Callistus escape—or die in the attempt.

CHAPTER XIV

Rome: One month later

Lucius

The teeming city seemed an unfriendly and squalid place after the open country I had traveled through to reach its gates. I had no friends here, all of my family and loved ones being in Capua, many miles away. I knew only of one man who might possibly still be in the city or nearby—Flavius. But how in the world could I ever find him? And if I did, would he again entertain the idea of helping me rescue Callistus?

My enquiries as to what had become of the big Gaul taken hostage by the Senate brought me the answers I most needed. Yes, he was still imprisoned. He had been tried and sentenced to death in the arena.

I listened, appalled. The Senate had gone back on its word. They had assured Brennus they would not execute Callistus, and now they had rescinded that promise. The sentence was to be carried out in one week's time, presided over by the entire Senate and many of the generals who had fought in Gaul. Sweet revenge for them, I thought bitterly. The only way they could see him defeated was to pit him against every gladiator in Rome. But even then, I thought with some relish, even then he will not die easily. He will take the best Rome can offer with him!

If it came to that…

I took lodgings at an *insula* near the arena in the hope that I might hear more of him from the vendors of the many stalls that stood in the shadow of the arena walls, or the customers that flocked to the countless taverns in the nearby streets.

There were rumors of course. He had killed six—or was it ten?—guards, trying to escape. They had shackled him to his cell wall to restrain him for he was like a wild beast, biting and clawing at anyone who came close. One man told me that the Senate had ordered he would face a hundred gladiators in the arena.

Even I thought that one a bit much. "Surely not a hundred?" I exclaimed, chuckling.

"Well, twenty perhaps…" The man was quick to change his far-fetched story.

"Ah, twenty," I said, straight-faced. "That might just do it, if they all rushed him at once."

My informant regarded me with wide eyes. "You know of this man?"

"I know of him, yes, from the battlefields of Gaul, and from the arenas of Capua. He will not die easily," I added, though it hurt me to say it.

"All of Rome will be there to see him die," said the purveyor of rumors.

And that rumor I believed.

"Lucius!" I heard my name called as I trod a desultory path through the market place. "By all the gods, Lucius!"

I turned to face the beaming smile of Tribune Flavius Sedonius.

"Flavius," I exclaimed, accepting his embrace of greeting. "But how dignified you look." He was wearing a white toga bordered in purple—the toga of a Senator.

"So much has happened since we last spoke, Lucius."

"You're a Senator," I pointed out needlessly.

"Yes…" His eyes clouded as he looked at my grim expression. "I am sorry, Lucius. I voted against his death sentence—the only dissenting vote I'm afraid."

"Thank you for that, at least," I said. "I am here to rescue him. Will you help me?"

He blinked at me. "You must know that is impossible. He is guarded night and day. The Senate is determined he will not escape punishment this time. He has humiliated them too often for them to take any chance he might escape."

"Nevertheless, you know I must try. He would do the same for me, you know that, Flavius."

He nodded. "Yes, I know that." He put his hand on my elbow and steered me away from the crowded marketplace. "I have a carriage nearby. Come with me to my villa and we will talk of this more—away from prying eyes and ears. Rome is full of spies these days it seems."

I let myself be led to his carriage. I trusted Flavius, even if he could not, or would not, help me, and in truth I was glad of his familiar company.

"You look well," I told him as I sat beside him. He had put on weight, and it gave him the air of the politician, rather than the fighting man I had known. "How is your father?"

"He retired to his country estate near Pompeii. I have not seen him since I returned from Gaul."

"You are estranged?"

"He cannot quite forgive me for siding with Egnatius."

"And General Egnatius?"

"Also retired. It was that or debasement, stripped of all his credits and pension."

"I wish I could feel some sympathy for either one of them," I said. "But I cannot."

"I understand…" He cocked his side to one side and smiled. "You might find the arrangement at the villa somewhat unconventional."

"How so?"

"I share my life with another man. His name is Julius."

"I am happy for you, Flavius," I said, and meant it. "Callistus and I shared a life in Gaul until treachery and Roman hubris took him from me again." I did not mean to sound quite so bitter, and said so, quickly apologizing.

"I understand," Flavius murmured, touching my hand. "I only wish there was something we could do."

"Could you arrange for me to see him?" I asked.

He frowned and shifted uncomfortably in his seat. "Not a good idea, Lucius. You would be seen as an accomplice to his crimes."

"Crimes?" I glared at him. "He is not a criminal, he is a warrior, and a prince! Treating him like some common criminal is Rome's way of debasing him. But I tell you this, Flavius, he will not be broken!"

"Hush, Lucius. Such talk will get you arrested."

"If that meant I could share his cell, I would welcome it."

The villa shared by Flavius and Julius, situated in one of Rome's richer districts, was fine indeed. Julius was handsome; he and Flavius made a striking couple and seemed to have the respect of their servants. There was an air of calm and well-being surrounding the villa and its occupants, and I could only envy what they had managed to obtain—a life together without fear of arrest or reprisal. Something I had concluded Callistus and I would never have.

Julius, of course, had been apprised by Flavius of my relationship with Callistus. I'm sure we were the subjects of many late night conversations between the two of them. As we sat over a cup of honeyed wine, Flavius took great delight in telling Julius how I had persuaded him to enlist me in the Roman army. If Julius was at all resentful of Flavius and me engaging in some carnality, he hid it well behind an amused expression. He too, I thought, would make a good politician.

"My only thought now," I told them, "is in how I can help Callistus escape the punishment the Senate has decreed."

Julius raised his finely shaped eyebrows in surprise. "There is not a man in Rome could make them change their mind, Lucius," he said. "Callistus is scheduled to die in the arena the day after tomorrow. The Senate's business is cancelled for the whole of that day so that all members can attend."

Hot tears welled in my eyes. "Why do they hate him so much? He was simply defending his homeland from invasion."

"He is seen as a threat to Rome, Lucius," Flavius said gently. "You know how prisoners of war are dealt with."

"Some are shown mercy," I interrupted. "King Brennus said the Senate had assured him Callistus would not receive the death penalty."

"A promise easily broken, I'm afraid," Julius said, summoning a servant to refill our cups. "Callistus has actually become a symbol of all that is weak within the military. Because of him our legions were forced to retreat and two of our revered generals forced into retirement. His death will be seen as befitting someone who would heap disgrace upon the Roman army."

I hung my head in despair. "He must die because of other's ineptitude?"

"I'm afraid that's about the sum of it," Julius said.

That night, although I had a fine bed to sleep upon, being a guest at the villa, I could not rest. Thoughts of what awaited Callistus in the arena plagued my mind and kept me awake until cock-crow. And desperately as I tried, I could think of no way for me to effect his release, or to even see him before the fateful day when he would be led into the arena to face the swords of those chosen to end his life.

"Oh, Callistus," I moaned as I sank back down on the bed, staring up at the ceiling. "If I could but see your face again, hold you in my arms… I would give everything, including my life, for that one moment."

✖ ✖ ✖ ✖ ✖

Later, dizzy from lack of sleep, I thanked my hosts and told them I must be on my way. I could not stay, surrounded by such luxury, while the man I longed for was chained and shackled in some dank cell awaiting death.

"But where will you go?" Flavius asked, frowning. "You know there is nothing you can do to save him."

"I know, but I must be closer to him," I replied. "Perhaps there is some way I could get into the place where they hold the prisoners..."

"Lucius!" Flavius grabbed my by my shoulders. "Don't even think of attempting such a thing. You will be arrested and perhaps share the same fate as Callistus."

I met his eyes squarely. "That is all I could ever hope for, Flavius. Without him, I will pray for death every day."

"Stop this. You are a young man. Your life's journey is still in front of you."

"To tread it alone, without him? I fear that is a journey I don't wish to make."

"Oh, Lucius..." Flavius had tears in his eyes as he stared at me. "Don't do anything rash, I beg you."

I shrugged. "We are all in the hands of the gods, Flavius. Their will must be mine also." I hugged him to me. "I would ask a favor."

"Of course."

"Lend me a horse."

"A horse?" His eyes searched my face for a moment or two. I could tell he was wondering what madness I was now planning. "Very well," he said finally. "But Lucius, whatever you do, do not try to enter the arena cells. No one who is taken there ever comes out alive."

The streets around the arena were teeming with activity when I arrived back at my room. There was an old stable at the back of the building where I could tether the horse Flavius had given me. He was an older steed, but strong and uncomplaining. I fed him some oats from the bin, then went for a walk, surveying the high walls of the arena and the many small doors the various vendors used. All of them were guarded, if not on the outside then most certainly within.

There was an event in progress, the last of the week until the spectacle the Senate had planned for Callistus. I paid my admission and walked up onto the stands surrounding the sanded floor of the arena. Two combatants were swinging at each other without much heart in it and the crowd was bored and restless. A far cry from when Callistus and Spartacus were face to face in the arena at Capua. That was a gladiatorial display to end them all—two magnificent men locked in deadly combat, each assured of his own prowess, and each respectful of his opponent's skill.

As I watched this less-than-stellar performance before me, I became aware of some activity near my side of the arena. Two young men had entered through a door set in the arena wall, ready to help a wounded gladiator—or carry a dead one—into the holding area beyond. I sidled nearer until I was able to see a gap in the wall where those who had business being there could enter and exit. I had no business being there, but I kept an eye on the young men, who looked as bored as the spectators and who were conversing in loud voices, not paying much attention to what was going on around them

Could I sneak past them? But just then a great shout went up from the crowd, drawing my eyes to where the gladiators were fighting. One of them had suddenly had a spurt of energy, bashing away at his opponent with his battle ax, driving the other man back across the sand. The two young men by the door also turned their attention to the action in front of them, and I moved into the gap to their side, inching my way toward them. A great roar went up, but I could not see what was happening. I was within a few feet of the door, one more distraction and I could very easily slip through unseen. Then one of them turned and saw me. I froze, but he grabbed me by the arm

"Come on," he yelled. "Give us a hand with the big one. He's got to weigh a ton or more!" He pulled me along to where one of the gladiators was lying flat on his back, a great bloody gash across his chest where the other man's sword had cut him.

"He's a goner," the young man next to me said. "Grab his feet, we'll take an arm apiece, and heave!" We staggered with the dead man between us toward the door which had been flung open. Inside, I almost gagged from the stench of blood and feces.

"Over there!" someone yelled and we deposited the body on the stone floor. The two youngsters, without a second look at me, ran back outside, waiting for the next bout. I was left alone in the dingy, stinking room without a clue as to what to do next. Was I anywhere near where I wanted to be? There was a passageway leading away from the room, and as it was the only exit apart from the one back into the arena, I ran to it. Ahead of me I could hear the wailing of frightened people, and the muted roar of some wild beast. I shuddered, wondering how anyone could spend their lives working in such a terrible place.

I rounded a corner at the end of the passageway and almost ran into a brute of a man who glared at me from one eye. The other was glued shut from a mixture of blood and pus. His bare chest was a mass of cuts and welts.

"A curse on you," he muttered. "Leaving me unattended. My eye needs attention, and you just up and left me!"

"You have me mistaken for someone else," I told him, taking his arm and turning him round in the direction from whence he came. "But show me where you were waiting and I'll fetch the physician."

"Huh," he grumbled, but shuffled along beside me complacently enough.

"What happened to your eye?"

"Isn't it obvious? A dirty trick from that bastard Greek who thinks he's the darling of the arena."

I had no idea who he was speaking of, but keeping hold of his arm I pushed him along until I heard voices ahead of us.

"I think we've found the physician," I said, and as I did so a young bearded man appeared carrying a bowl of water.

"Ah, there you are Crassus," he said. "Why did you wander off like that?"

"He was a little lost," I said, handing Crassus over. "I'm glad we found you." Before the physician could say more, I slipped past them, down another long passageway. I was well and truly lost, but thought if I just kept on till I found the holding cells, I would at least be somewhere close to finding Callistus.

"Hey, you!" My blood froze at the sound of the rough voice. I turned to see two guards approaching. I was on the verge of running when my better instincts took control and I waited, my expression blank as they came near.

"What are you doing down here?" one of them asked.

"I'm an assistant to the physician," I lied. "But I seem to have lost my way. Not too difficult in this maze."

"You've been busy," the other guard said, prodding my chest. I looked down at the large bloodstain on my tunic. Crassus must have bled on me when I was escorting him.

"Yes," I said. "Lots of blood today."

"That's what the crowd likes to see. So where do you need to be?"

"At the holding cells. One of the prisoners is calling for a physician. My master is too busy, so he sent me." I was secretly amazed at how creative I had suddenly become with my lies.

The first guard grunted and pointed the length of the passageway. "Down to the end, first left, then right. There'll be someone there to let you know where you're needed."

"Thank you, officer." I turned, and tried not to run in my haste to get away before they might guess I was not anyone's assistant. I could practically feel their eyes upon my back as I hurried down the passageway. When no shout sounded from behind me, I breathed a sigh of relief. Ahead, the holding cells teemed with miserable wretches, all moaning and crying out for help from the gods or their mothers. *What a hellish place to end up in*, I thought, searching each cell as I passed for any sign of Callistus. So many times a whimpering soul would reach out a hand to me in supplication, a silent pleading for help I could not give.

It was obvious that Callistus was not among these prisoners. Where else could they have taken him? And how much longer could I remain here without being discovered, questioned, and perhaps myself locked up? A door at the end of the passageway caught my attention. I ran to it and pushed against it. It opened with surprising ease and revealed a long flight of steps descending into what looked like a pit of darkness. But as I peered into the gloom and my eyes grew accustomed to the lack of light, I could see two cell doors off to one side. There was no sign of a guard, probably indicating it was felt there was no need, yet here I was, most definitely where I should not be.

Carefully, I descended the steps, listening for any sound that might indicate a nearby hidden guard, but I heard nothing. The first door was slightly open, the cell empty. The second was locked, and my heart raced as I peered through the grill at the top of the door, and saw a tall figure shackled to the wall.

"Callistus!" I hissed. "It is I, Lucius!"

He raised his head and my stomach shrank at the sight of his face, so beaten, cut and bruised as to be almost unrecognizable. A terrible anger gripped me. That they could do this to the man I loved and revered above all others. If I could lay my hands on those responsible I would kill them, and enjoy every moment of their pain before they died.

The man who now came upon me at that very moment was the one to feel the full brunt of my anger.

"Hey," he shouted at me. "What are you...?"

That was as far as he got. With a snarling sound I had never before in my life uttered I fell upon him, beating him unmercifully until he fell to the ground, where I then pounded his head against the stone slabs until the blood ran and he lay still. I leaned over him, my breath rasping in my chest. It was not until I began to push myself to my feet that I saw the bunch of keys at his waist. With a trembling hand I inserted one, then another, then another into the lock until, the gods be praised, the latch turned and the door swung open.

"Lucius," Callistus groaned through swollen lips. "You must not do this. If they find you here they will kill you."

"Hush, my love," I whispered, trying to find the key to unlock his shackles. "You think I could stand idly by while you suffered like this? I have a horse stabled nearby. All we have to do is get out of here."

Despite his pain, a dry chuckle escaped his chest. "Yes, that's all we have to do…"

He almost collapsed onto the cell floor as I unlocked the chains that held him to the wall. I supported him, putting his arm around my shoulders, my arm about his waist. He was bloodied, filthy, and stank of his own excrement, but I cared for none of that. I kissed his cheek as he leaned on me and we started for the door. I had no idea in Hades how we were to escape detection and find a way out, but I had come this far, and there was no alternative now but to press on.

"That door there," Callistus said, gesturing weakly. "That's the one they brought me through from the outside."

I kicked at it and it creaked open and we both gasped at the rush of cool air that swept over us. "We must be very near the outside walls," I muttered, looking down the long deserted corridor leading from the doorway. "Let's see how far we can get." I could only hope that no other guard came to discover the one I had killed. If no alarm was raised we had a good chance of either finding somewhere to hide until nightfall, or getting out through one of the vendor doors. As we rounded a corner, I drew us both back hastily. Ahead, men were unloading sacks of sand for the arena from carts stationed outside. The sacks were being piled into stacks, and apart from the men unloading the carts there seemed to be no one else in attendance. Not one of them glanced our way as they went about their business with an air of resigned drudgery.

"Stay here," I whispered to Callistus, an idea forming in my mind. I walked forward, head down, and grabbed a sack from one of the carts, throwing it down on top of the others. It was the practice of vendors to recruit men as they were needed for heavy work. These men had probably been hanging around looking for just such work to earn a denarius or two. My being in their midst would not give them a moment's pause.

When all the carts were emptied and began to pull away, I stayed by the door. "I'll close up," I said to the men with some air of authority while keeping my face averted from them. Better that they did not recall me should they later be questioned. No one argued and I banged the door shut behind them. I waited a minute or two, but did not want to remain any longer than we had to for fear someone came to inspect the delivery. I ran to where Callistus still stood, leaning on the wall for support.

"When I open the door, we will be outside the arena near the marketplace," I told him. "My room is nearby. Once you have rested, we can leave the city at night on the horse Flavius gave me. Now…" I put his arms across my shoulders again. "Pretend to be drunk once we're outside. Just lean on me…"

"Lucius," he murmured.

"Later, my love, speak later. Right now conserve your strength for the ordeal ahead."

Slowly, we made our way through the door and out into the bustling marketplace. *So*, I thought, *we have come this far. May the gods keep smiling on us*. Few took much notice as I guided my ragged and filthy companion through the market. Drunks and beggars were commonplace in Rome. Victims of robberies, or down and outs in need of food and shelter rarely received any attention—and that is what I now relied on. Despite not having had any clear cut plan, I had managed the impossible—now I could only pray that our luck held.

CHAPTER XV

Amazingly, we made it to my room without being stopped or even eyed suspiciously. I wondered how many of the people we had passed would remember us when the hue and cry went up at the discovery of Callistus' escape. Once inside my room, I helped Callistus lie upon my cot then I stripped him of the filthy rags he wore. His magnificent body was covered in cuts, bruises and the marks of the lash. I could tell by the white crust on his skin that the only attention his wounds had received was having salt water thrown over him.

After I had given him fresh water to drink, I bathed him with warm water and a soft cloth, wishing I had some soothing balm with which to treat the many cuts on his body and face. All the while I ministered to him his eyes never closed, never left my face. At one point he took my hand and raised it to his bruised lips. My eyes filled with tears as I bent to kiss him.

"Lucius..." His voice, weak though it was, held love for me, and my heart melted at the sound. "The gods have made you mad."

Well, not exactly the words I had wanted to hear, but I smiled and kissed him again. "The madness you imbue me with my love," I murmured against his lips. "The madness that when we are safely away from here, and you are fully recovered, I will let you tame me of with the stamina only you possess."

He smiled, then closed his eyes. I let him sleep, for in truth we could go no further without him regaining at least some of his strength. When his empty cell was discovered and the search for him began, we would be safer here in my room than out on the streets. No doubt, a door to door search would eventually be conducted, but I would find some way of dealing with that when it happened. Until then he would rest, and I would protect him with my life.

We needed food, perhaps some wine, and I had to know what had happened in the hours since our escape from the arena prison cells. Callistus slept peacefully, for which I was grateful as I slipped from my room. It was only a short walk to the marketplace where I could purchase bread, cheese and some fruit.

I would like to have procured some balm for his wounds, but I was half afraid that I might arise some suspicion in the apothecary's mind if I, without a scratch on me, asked for ointments of any kind.

"A quiet day," I remarked to the baker as he handed over a loaf of bread.

He nodded. "Considering what has happened, yes it is."

"What has happened?" I enquired, stone faced.

"The Gaul who was to have died in the arena tomorrow has escaped after murdering twelve guards!"

"*Twelve guards*?" I barely managed to stifle the guffaw that threatened to burst from my lips. "He must be quite a fighter."

"Probably crept up on all of them unawares," the baker groused.

"Still, twelve of them," I marveled. "Perhaps it's just as well they didn't set him loose in the arena."

"They'll catch him in no time."

I looked around. "But where are the search parties, the guards going from door to door?"

"Someone said they saw him on a cart heading for the gates. They're already searching outside the city."

Praise the gods! I silently exulted. Who could that highly imaginative person have been? I would like to find him or her and kiss them soundly!

After more purchases from stalls where the story was more or less the same, except that the number of bodies Callistus had left behind increased with each telling.

"Twenty guards!" I stared at the wine merchant in amazement. "The Gaul must be a monster indeed!"

I made a hasty retreat back to my room, hoping that Callistus was in a fit state to receive my news of his killing prowess. I found him awake and sitting up on the bed. Although it would take time for all his wounds to heal properly, much to my relief he already looked better. He stood as I entered, a little shakily, but with a determined smile on his lips. I laid my purchases on the table and stepped into his arms, carefully holding his naked body with the gentlest of caresses.

"My Lucius," he murmured, his lips pressed to my hair. "The bravest of all men I have known."

"Not the maddest?" I teased, kissing his chest.

His azure eyes met mine with a tender look. "The bravest," he said. "I can think of no other who would have done what you dared to do."

"I know of one other," I replied. "You, should I have been in your position."

He sighed, his breath warm on my brow. "That is true." He tilted my face to his and kissed my lips. "Nothing will ever part us, Lucius, but death itself."

"Let us not talk of death, when life has been given to us again," I said, returning his kiss. "Now, do you feel like you could eat something? It's only bread and cheese, but I also brought some wine."

Callistus smiled. "After the slop they gave me to barely keep me alive, that sounds like ambrosia from the gods."

"Come then and sit at the table," I urged him. "Afterward I will fetch water to fill the tub so you may bathe properly. The building has a bath, but I fear you might be in danger should anyone get suspicious of who you might be."

He nodded as he tore off a chunk of bread from the loaf. "I might be recognized. They marched me through the streets upon my arrival."

I felt my anger return at the thought of his humiliation. "I wish a plague upon the Senate—except for Flavius. His was the one vote against your sentence of death, and he loaned me the horse which we will use to return to Gaul."

"He is now a Senator?"

"Yes, and he lives with his lover, Julius, in a villa on the outskirts of the city."

"I am glad he has found happiness." He caressed my face with his fingertips. "I wish I could bring that same happiness to you, Lucius."

I kissed his fingertips. "Believe me, my love, when I say you do. A greater happiness I could not ask for."

✵   ✵   ✵   ✵   ✵

After a sound night's sleep, the next morning brought even more strength to Callistus. A natural healer, the shallower cuts on his body had already scabbed over, while the lash marks, though red and angry, did not appear to be infected. We decided that after one more day he would be fit to travel. In the meantime I would find Flavius and ask for one more favor. Some clothes and money to last enough for our journey to Gaul. I had but the tunic I stood in, and Callistus had not even that, using a sheet from the bed to cover his nakedness from time to time. Never had a prince been so beggared, and though it angered me to see him thus, he bore it with the dignity befitting his royal blood.

Thankfully, Flavius was at home when I called upon him. Of course, he knew of Callistus' escape, even though he had not been in the city since I last saw him.

"The Senate is in an uproar, Lucius," he said, after embracing me warmly. "I, of course, have nothing to tell them that might aid the army in its search." He winked at me. "However did you do it?"

"The gods made me invisible," I said with a straight face. "And gave me the luck only they can bestow. I need another favor of you, Flavius."

"Anything."

"We have no money, nor does Callistus have anything to wear. The rags I found him in I had to destroy."

"I will provide you with some woolen clothing," Flavius said. "Winter is almost upon us, the going will be difficult, Lucius."

"But we cannot delay," I told him. "Every day we spend in Rome brings us the danger of discovery."

"You're right, but Lucius, your troubles do not end there." Flavius put his hand on my shoulder and steered me toward the villa. "The Senate convenes late tonight to discuss the latest upheaval in Gaul."

"What d'you mean?"

"King Brennus of the Saquini has employed mercenaries to aid him in his attempt to overthrow Callistus' uncle, King Banthius. With Callistus gone, Brennus deems it an easy task. Banthius is old and cannot lead his men into battle. He relied on Callistus for that."

"But he has other men who can lead," I protested. "Perhaps not as skillfully as Callistus, but at least well enough to fend off a challenge from the Saquini. What I saw of their battle readiness was not impressive."

"That is why Brennus is using mercenaries," Flavius said patiently. "The Senate is awaiting the outcome before deciding on Rome's next move."

I sighed. "Will this never end, Flavius? Sometimes I wish I could spirit Callistus away to some far-off land where we could live the rest of our days in peace."

"A warrior prince living in peace, Lucius? Not until he can no longer wield his sword in defense of his country. Your fantasy of finding some quiet haven where you can both live out your lives in tranquility is no more than a pipe dream, I'm afraid."

Callistus received the news I brought from Flavius with a grim nod. "I should have known better than to trust Brennus," he said bitterly. "Part of our agreement when I offered to give myself up to the Romans was that he would not attempt an invasion of Helvetii land. He cannot yet have learned of my escape, so his plans are all the more heinous." He gripped my arm tightly. "We must return to Gaul at all speed, Lucius. My uncle will need me more than ever now."

✖ ✖ ✖ ✖ ✖

We set off the following day. Dressed in the clothes Flavius had given us, and with a cloak thrown over his head to hide his blond hair, Callistus sat astride the horse while I led it through the gates. The guards hardly gave us a glance, so busy were they watching some girls dressed only in gossamer skirts, engaged in an exotic dance. The musical tinkling of the tiny cymbals they wore on their fingers and toes lent a happy sound to the hammering of my heart as we passed by the guards.

Once away from the immediate danger of arrest, Callistus bade me climb up on the horse in front of him. He wrapped his arms around me and prodded the steed into a sharp canter across the meadows that flanked the Appian Way. We had agreed it was better to avoid the roads as much as possible while we were still within a day or two of the city.

✖ ✖ ✖ ✖ ✖

CALLISTUS

Time and time again I marveled at my lover's bravery. I had always thought Lucius daring and headstrong, but what he had managed to do in the past few days was nothing short of miraculous. I could think of many trained warriors who could not have carried out what he did. Time and again I cursed myself for putting his life in danger. My stupidity in thinking that I could trust Brennus or the Roman Senate still sat like a thorn in my mind. And now, because of my foolhardiness, my country was in danger of being seized by Brennus, with the aid of mercenaries—and ultimately by Rome. Such a thing I could not allow, and if by my actions my people were made to suffer, I would move heaven and earth to make amends.

As we began our journey it seemed as though the gods were still with us. We encountered no Roman search parties scouting for us, and the weather held cool days leading to cooler nights, when we would lie in the shelter of each other's arms, wrapped in the blankets Flavius had provided.

We had been without a loving closeness since I left Lucius in Saquini territory, he being afraid to aggravate my wounds, but now lying with him in my arms I felt the fire in my blood and in my loins that only his nearness could bring me. Only his kisses could inflame my body and soul with a passion that would remain unabated 'til he brought me release.

"Lucius," I whispered, my lips on his. "My need for you is too great to ignore. Let me make love to you."

With a willing sigh he pressed his warm, smooth body to mine, taking my lips with his. His breath was sweet upon my tongue, his cock as hard as iron between my thighs. He moved over me, the caresses from his lips and fingers light and as gentle as thistle down.

"Don't think that you will cause me pain," I complained. "I want to feel your hands press on my flesh, your lips take mine as you want. I am not an invalid, Lucius."

"Your body is still bruised and the welts from the lash still angry," he said softly, his lips on mine. "I will not bring you pain with my love, Callistus. Just let me do it my way. You will love it, you'll see."

Ignoring my grumbling, he trailed a path of kisses over my torso, lingering over each nipple, teasing those parts of me only he had power over, the power to inflame me with a burning, sensual excitement that always threatened to take me over the edge too quickly. But only he knew just how much to give, and when to ease up as he now did, hearing my breathing quicken in my chest. His smile as he raised his head and gazed into my eyes was enough to make me want to ravish him on the spot, but I resisted on seeing the warning glint in his eyes. He lowered his head again, and this time ventured further south toward that part of me that now begged for his mouth.

"Mmm..." His murmur of appreciation as he engulfed my aching cock with the moist warmth of his mouth was followed by the sound of the loudest gasp I have ever heard escape my lips. A gasp that was really a groan, a groan that was more of a plea; a plea that could only be answered by my lover, my Lucius, who now laved my hard flesh with his lips and tongue, catching me up in a tumult of desire and lust like no other man, or woman, ever could. He sucked until my mind and body could no longer bear the ecstasy, and I pulled him up into my arms to bathe his face with my kisses while his body writhed over me, inflaming both of us with a hungry desire.

He sat astride me, reaching behind himself to grasp my cock made slick with his saliva. He eased himself upon my shaft, taking all of me inside him, the flicker of pain on his face soon erased by the wanton smile I loved to see when we made love. He began a slow and steady rhythm, up and down on my rigid cock while his hands caressed my body, gently avoiding the worst of the healing cuts. I grasped his hands and pressed them to my flesh, caring not for the pain, only wanting to feel the firm pressure of his hands on me. Smiling, he leaned forward to take my mouth with his, his tongue sliding between my parted lips bringing me sensations that only he could. My hips rose to drive my cock deeper, all the way inside the silky heat of his core. He groaned into my mouth and I held him locked in my arms, our bodies now moving together completely as one. I felt his breath quicken, signaling his imminent orgasm and I plunged harder, faster to join him. We came together with gasping cries of joy and delirious release. The streams of semen torn from both our bodies bore witness to how long it had been since we had last taken carnal pleasure in one another.

And afterward, while we lay in each other's embrace, and the whispered words of love and commitment were stilled by sleep, my dreams took Lucius and I to another place where men such as we live and love as warriors, side by side, forever.

Epilogue

Lucius

The armies were drawn against one another: Brennus of the Saquini leading his mercenaries on one side, Callistus of the Helvetii with his force of loyal warriors on the other. Side by side, astride our steeds, Callistus and I waited for the enemy to make their move. The ground beneath our horses' hooves was hard and cold as stone, while around us flurries of snow blurred our vision. Not the ideal conditions for engaging the enemy, but there was no going back now, no giving ground. Brennus had challenged the sovereignty of the Helvetii. That challenge had been met and the future of both tribes would be decided by this last battle.

In the intervening months since our return to his homeland, Callistus had tried again and again to forge a peace with Brennus, the Saquini king, but to no avail. Brennus thought he had rid himself of Callistus once and for all, and without him, the land of the Helvetii would be his—poorly defended and ready to secede to his sovereignty. When the news was brought to Brennus that Callistus had not died in a Roman arena and had returned home, it is said he fell into a wild rage, even cursing his Roman allies and demanding that they support him in his determination to bring Callistus to his knees. That support had not materialized, and it was rumored that the Roman Senate had not even replied to the king's demands.

Despite Callistus' attempts to bring reason to Brennus, and despite also his military advisors telling him a truce with Callistus would not cause him to lose face, Brennus had gone against the will of his people, hiring a mercenary army to aid him in his quest for power over the Helvetii.

For weeks now there had been raids and skirmishes involving both sides, but our spies had reported that the mercenaries were not content with the paltry booty they captured when they were successful. Their leaders wanted gold, and had urged Brennus to take this greater step in his bid to vanquish the Helvetii. Rather than lose his paid allies, he had chosen this place to make good on his challenge.

As I reined in my restless steed, I thought how far away Capua now seemed. Not just in distance measured in miles, but in my thoughts and in my heart. I was certain I would never see my family again, nor my friends Petronius and Turio. My life was now centered on my love and loyalty to my prince. He alone governed my deeds, my actions and my heart.

Callistus turned to me and smiled. "When this day is over, Lucius," he said, "you and I will sit by the fire with a cup of warmed wine and talk of the bravery of this army."

I returned his smile and nodded my agreement. "And of how King Brennus groveled at your feet, begging forgiveness for his treachery—if he still lives after the battle."

Ahead, the sound of marching feet, cantering horses and the clinking of armor heralded the approach of Brennus' forces.

"Archers!" Callistus called out. "Front and center, and wait for my signal."

A mass of men ran into formation in front of us, stretching their bows in readiness for their prince's orders. The Helvetii archers were a formidable force, capable of bringing down charging horsemen and heavily armored soldiers. The iron-tipped shafts could even penetrate shields at long range. These men were Callistus' main offense against the enemy, with the rest of us on horseback as the second assault.

The sounds of marching came loudly to our ears across the frozen landscape.

"Archers, ready!"

Callistus raised his arm, his eyes straining to see through the thickening snow. The archers bent their bows, pointing their arrows into the black sky.

"Now!"

The whoosh of hundreds of arrows filling the air was followed shortly by the screams and groans of men felled by the lethal barrage that struck unseen through the blinding snow.

"Archers ready!"

And again those deadly shafts rained down on an enemy we still could barely see. Screams of men and the whinnying of wounded horses rent the air, and then as the archers fell back behind us, Callistus gave the order to charge.

I spurred my horse forward, anxious to keep as close to Callistus as I could. I had the unnerving sensation of riding into a void, for I could see nothing but a thick white veil in front of me. Had there been an abyss before us, we surely all would have plunged over the edge. Fortunately we had scouted the land before us earlier in the day, and so I galloped on, knowing no such pitfalls lay ahead, only the enemy, thrown into disarray by the archers.

Callistus' riders crashed through the first line of defense, laying waste to the few soldiers still standing, then on to where Brennus' cavalry awaited his orders. Too late, it seemed, for we were upon them, slashing and hacking and driving them back in disorder. And then, praise to all the gods, the snow stopped abruptly, only a few flakes blowing into my face, while a faint wintry sliver of sunlight revealed the carnage around us.

Everywhere the dead lay where they had been struck down by the Helvetii archers, and more toppled from their horses by our charge. The survivors immediately lost heart and scattered across the frozen plain in all directions. Callistus called a halt to the killing and allowed no man to chase down the fleeing mercenaries. We found Brennus lying on his back, impaled by an arrow through his chest.

There would be no groveling for mercy from the Saquini king.

Our return was greeted by the people with joy, and after Callistus had reported to his uncle of our victory, he was true to his word. We spent the night by the fireside, drinking warmed wine and talking of the bravery of his army. As another fall of snow blanketed the countryside, he took me into the warmth of his arms, and I, rejoicing that for the present the danger was past, made love to him and he to me, over and over 'til the first light of cold dawn stole through the shuttered windows.

Before sleep finally overtook us, we pledged that no matter what occurred, our love for each other would be resolute and true. The future is at best uncertain, and in these times filled with danger and the threat of betrayal. But for now, and indeed 'til death takes one or both of us, we two will be as constant and unchanging as the heavens above us.

About the Author

J.P. BOWIE was born and raised in Aberdeen, Scotland. He wrote his first (unpublished) novel at the age of 14 - a science fiction tale of brawny men and brawnier women that made him a little suspect in the eyes of his family for a while.

J.P. wrote his first gay mystery in 2000, and after having it rejected by every publisher in the universe, he opted to put his money where his mouth is and self published *A Portrait of Phillip*. Now several books, short stories and novellas later, he is writing m/m erotica almost exclusively. J.P.'s favorite singer is Ella Fitzgerald, and his favorite man is Phil, his partner of 15 years. Visit J.P. on the internet at http://www.jpbowie.com.

THE TREVOR PROJECT

The Trevor Project operates the only nationwide, around-the-clock crisis and suicide prevention helpline for lesbian, gay, bisexual, transgender and questioning youth. Every day, The Trevor Project saves lives though its free and confidential helpline, its website and its educational services. If you or a friend are feeling lost or alone call The Trevor Helpline. If you or a friend are feeling lost, alone, confused or in crisis, please call The Trevor Helpline. You'll be able to speak confidentially with a trained counselor 24/7.

The Trevor Helpline: 866-488-7386

On the Web: http://www.thetrevorproject.org/

THE GAY MEN'S DOMESTIC VIOLENCE PROJECT

Founded in 1994, The Gay Men's Domestic Violence Project is a grassroots, non-profit organization founded by a gay male survivor of domestic violence and developed through the strength, contributions and participation of the community. The Gay Men's Domestic Violence Project supports victims and survivors through education, advocacy and direct services. Understanding that the serious public health issue of domestic violence is not gender specific, we serve men in relationships with men, regardless of how they identify, and stand ready to assist them in navigating through abusive relationships.

GMDVP Helpline: 800.832.1901

On the Web: http://gmdvp.org/

THE GAY & LESBIAN ALLIANCE AGAINST DEFAMATION/GLAAD EN ESPAÑOL

The Gay & Lesbian Alliance Against Defamation (GLAAD) is dedicated to promoting and ensuring fair, accurate and inclusive representation of people and events in the media as a means of eliminating homophobia and discrimination based on gender identity and sexual orientation.

On the Web: http://www.glaad.org/

GLAAD en español:

http://www.glaad.org/espanol/bienvenido.php

SERVICEMEMBERS LEGAL DEFENSE NETWORK

Servicemembers Legal Defense Network is a nonpartisan, nonprofit, legal services, watchdog and policy organization dedicated to ending discrimination against and harassment of military personnel affected by "Don't Ask, Don't Tell" (DADT).The SLDN provides free, confidential legal services to all those impacted by DADT and related discrimination. Since 1993, its inhouse legal team has responded to more than 9,000 requests for assistance. In Congress, it leads the fight to repeal DADT and replace it with a law that ensures equal treatment for every servicemember, regardless of sexual orientation. In the courts, it works to challenge the constitutionality of DADT.

SLDN
PO Box 65301
Washington DC 20035-5301
On the Web: http://sldn.org/

Call: (202) 328-3244
or (202) 328-FAIR
e-mail: sldn@sldn.org

THE GLBT NATIONAL HELP CENTER

The GLBT National Help Center is a nonprofit, tax-exempt organization that is dedicated to meeting the needs of the gay, lesbian, bisexual and transgender community and those questioning their sexual orientation and gender identity. It is an outgrowth of the Gay & Lesbian National Hotline, which began in 1996 and now is a primary program of The GLBT National Help Center. It offers several different programs including two national hotlines that help members of the GLBT community talk about the important issues that they are facing in their lives. It helps end the isolation that many people feel, by providing a safe environment on the phone or via the internet to discuss issues that people can't talk about anywhere else. The GLBT National Help Center also helps other organizations build the infrastructure they need to provide strong support to our community at the local level.

National Hotline: 1-888-THE-GLNH (1-888-843-4564)
National Youth Talkline 1-800-246-PRIDE (1-800-246-7743)
On the Web: http://www.glnh.org/
e-mail: info@glbtnationalhelpcenter.org

Stimulate yourself.
READ.

www.manloveromance.com
THE HOTTEST M/M EROTIC AUTHORS & WEBSITES ON THE NET